TALES FROM
THE HIDDEN NOTEBOOKS OF M R JAMES

FIVE GHOST STORIES

Edited by
Dr Edward Cowling

With the assistance of
John Joseph Denwood

Copyright

© John Joseph Denwood 2018

The moral right of John Joseph Denwood to be identified as the author of this work has been asserted

by him in accordance with the

Copyright, Designs and Patents Act of 1988

All rights reserved

This is a work of fiction

Cover photo of M R James courtesy of Wikimedia Commons

CONTENTS

Story	*Page*
Editor's Introduction	5
The Cellars of Ezekiel	7
The Hearties of Adonai	47
The Organ of Corpusty	79
The Island of Tyskär	115
The Bones of Paston	155

Editor's Introduction

Montague Rhodes James (1862 - 1936) was a distinguished scholar of early medieval literature, including the New Testament Apocrypha, and of the archaeological record of the same period.

His great accomplishments as an antiquarian led to his election as a Fellow of the British Academy and to the bestowal by King George V of the Order of Merit - the supreme honour for cultural achievement in the British Commonwealth.

Dr James was, in the course of his career, a Fellow of King's College, Cambridge, the Director of the Fitzwilliam Museum, the Provost of King's College, and finally the Provost of his old school, Eton.

James published innumerable scholarly works (including descriptive catalogues of the manuscripts held by ancient Cambridge colleges, and, in 1924, an outstanding edition of the New Testament Apocrypha), but also popular and highly readable volumes about historic buildings in the West Country, Suffolk and Norfolk. He is undoubtedly most famous, however, for his interest in the supernatural, which led him to pen some of finest ghost stories in the English language.

'Monty', as his friends called him, was non-committal on whether he actually believed in ghosts and demons. His only comment was that he was prepared to consider evidence, and accept it if it satisfied him. This judicious approach did not prevent him from writing gripping tales.

In 1918, Dr James left Cambridge to become Provost of Eton. He died in that post, and was buried in a simple grave in Eton Town Cemetery.

When the Old Provost's Lodge at King's was being restored in 1978, I was a doctoral student at that college, writing a thesis on the impact of the Reformation on the concept of the disembodied soul in Protestant countries. Already fascinated by James's interest in ghosts, I nipped into the Old Lodge late one afternoon, just after the workmen had gone, and looked around the rooms that the great man had occupied. A shaft of sunlight from the south-west suddenly entered the room I was in - it was, I think, his old bedroom - and lit up the plasterless chimney breast. This beam revealed a couple of bricks wholly devoid of mortar. I pulled the bricks out and found behind them a small cavity containing a stash of notebooks. I fished the books out with glee and, after a moment's inspection, saw that they appeared to have been written by the famous antiquarian himself.

What is supremely interesting about these notebooks - if, indeed, they are genuine, as I believe - is that from them one can extract coherent stories about M R James's own encounters with the occult. As I am now nearing death myself, I have decided to publish edited versions of the notebooks, each monograph dealing with one curious episode in the great scholar's life.

Edward Cowling
Fellow of All Angels College, Cambridge

Feast of the Transfiguration 2015

THE CELLARS OF EZEKIEL

Saturday 30th September 1899

I am reading a most amusing book, borrowed from the University Library, viz. the Reverend Reginald Rabett's *Latineos*, in which the poor fellow proves that the Pope in Rome is Antichrist because he is the man who speaks Latin!

Never have I seen the ancient tongues put to the service of such stupidity.

By Mr Rabett's reckoning, the Provost of Eton must be the Antichrist too - along with every other public and grammar school head master in the country.

The chap was at Queen's, it seems.

***

Sunday 1st October 1899

I have done a little more work on my catalogue of the manuscripts of Ezekiel College. As the second oldest foundation after Peterhouse, its collection is an inexhaustible delight. It's hardly surprising, with such a marvellous resource, that the college has acquired such a distinguished reputation for historical scholarship.

Today I finished reading Conybeare's paper in *Studia Biblica* on the Armenian text of *The Acts of Pilate*. His work strongly supports Tischendorf's Greek Recension A of Part I.

That charming youth, Philimore Argent, the junior organ scholar, played the great Passacaglia and Fugue in C Minor after Evensong. Old Sebastian Bach certainly knew how to build immense walls of sound.

As my ear followed the line of the fugue, so my eye followed the line of the vault above me. It's a long piece. The Provost was rather vexed. He was hungry, I expect.

There was a disagreeable episode at dinner. I was conversing with Barnabas Lamb, the Vice-Chaplain, about the influence of the Neo Platonists, and especially Plotinus, on Pseudo-Dionysius and Saint Augustine, when Eddie Nicholson, who was sitting opposite us, began to shout at me.

'You know full well that the Christian Faith is based purely and solely on the historical events attested to in the New Testament,' he bellowed, in his brawny Belfast accent, waving his greasy knife at me. He really is the worst kind of evangelical.

I took a sip of wine and said, 'Don't be ridiculous.'

But Nicholson was unreasonably angry. I suspect he dislikes me for reasons quite unconnected to my scholarly interest in heterodoxy. What they are, I can't imagine.

On the question of theological correctness, I have had occasion to note before that it is physicists and engineers (Dr Nicholson is an expert on steam engines) who are the most literal-minded.

So very tiresome. I shall have to avoid Nicholson for a week or two.

Deo adjuvante, non timendum.

Barnabas, as well as being a clergyman and a passable Greek scholar, is a mathematician of high calibre. His theology is subtler.

Poor dear Barney! He took the Irishman's explosion very badly. He immediately shrank back, hugging the waist band of his cassock as if for protection, his eyes fixed on the uneaten dauphinoise on the plate before him. Even before Dr Nicholson's outburst, he had already seemed to me to exude an air of anxiety over something indiscernible. But after dinner, he nevertheless invited me round to his rooms for Dessert.

I protested that he looked tired and that I'd be just as happy perusing a tale by Le Fanu.

'My dear Monty,' he smiled. 'I must insist.'

Barney sported a most refreshing pineapple as the centre piece of his table and produced a tawny port that was immodestly good for a young clergyman.

On the basis of the port, I made merry about his absurd title, naturally. Vice Chaplain! Poor Barney really ought to ask the Council to change it, especially as he's inherently and unalterably virtuous.

But that's by-the-by.

Best of all was a rather queer story that Barney brought to me from Ezekiel College. I could see that he was very nervous about telling it but also felt impelled to do so.

This is the gist of what he said:

'I don't know whether you ever talk much with your bedder,' he began (I could not prevent myself from shuddering at the mere thought of this), 'but mine's a shrewd old stick, and she keeps me pretty well informed about what's going on in college politics. The odd thing is that although she's been a servant of the college for years and years, she is actually very sympathetic to the ideas of the New King's men; and so the Etonians of the Best Set and the New Men alike both feel able to mention their ambitions and vexations to her. She's a Methodist herself and doesn't care much for the Established Church, but she respects my cloth, as she puts it, and passes on anything she thinks might be useful to me in doing "the Lord's work in the college".

'Well, a couple of days ago, she came to me and said, very solemnly, that she knew of a gentleman in great distress who might be glad of my ministrations. When I asked her for details, she explained that a very good friend of hers, a Mrs

Frior, was a bedder at Ezekiel, and that among this other lady's charges was a man called Potter, a Fellow of Ezekiel, and a medical man by profession. Potter had spent many years in East Africa, working as a medical missionary, and at the same time had played a major part in describing previously unknown tropical diseases. After a peaceful year or two at Ezekiel, during which he began new research into muscle degeneration and was elected Librarian of his college, he suddenly fell ill with a gruesome disease that his colleagues think he can only have contracted in Africa.

'His skin, it seems, has turned quite yellow, his eyes red, and he coughs up blood and lies quite incapacitated in his bed. The Master of the College, who is himself a distinguished medical man and a former Serjeant Surgeon to Her Majesty the Queen, has attended Dr Potter, and insists that the invalid needs only a prolonged period of quiet and rest in his own bed.

'Now, Mrs Frior, Dr Potter's bedder, has apparently said that she can't believe that nothing more can be done to relieve her gentleman's distress, and that Potter repeatedly asks her to get help. When she approached the college authorities at Ezekiel with this, they apparently became very angry and indignant at what they called her impertinence. Threatened with dismissal, she decided to opt for discretion. But Potter continued to press her to act on his behalf. When she asked the poor fellow who might be able to help him, he actually muttered your name, Monty, and asked for some paper.'

'My name?' I queried, removing the pipe from my mouth. 'But I've never heard of Dr Potter before, let alone met him.'

'Which apparently is why Mrs Frior approached Mrs Gull, my bedder, to ask if she could effect some kind of introduction through me. I'm sorry to bother you with the whole bizzare tale, Monty, but I felt that I couldn't really refuse - because of this.'

From a pocket of his cassock, he took out a folded sheet of paper, and held it out to me.

As I read the note, I could sense Barney's eyes glancing nervously around my face.

'Good Lord,' I murmured, 'this document's in Ethiopic. But hang on a minute, this isn't Ethiopic. Why, it's English written in the characters of the old language, that's all.'

'Mrs Gull said that she was sure you'd be able to help.'

'Is your bedder an expert on my *curriculum vitae*?'

'She said she was sure you're a charitable man.'

'This is a letter from Dr Potter to me. Or at least, it purports to be.'

'What does it say?'

'Hang on a moment. There are no vowels ... "my dear James, please excuse this ... note, but come and save me ... devil prowleth ... here ... as roaring lion ... help please". How extraordinary.'

'First Peter, Chapter 5, Verse 8,' muttered Barney.

I must have stared at him incredulously, for he began to blush.

'Oh, it was ridiculous of me to bring this to you,' he sighed.

'Not at all, not at all,' I said, as consolingly as I could.

'He sounds deranged,' muttered my friend.

I shook my head.

'Perhaps not,' I murmured.

'How do you mean?'

'There's something rather uncanny going on here. I have what on the face of it seems a very relevant confession to make.'

'A confession?'

'I was looking through an original copy of Martin Luther's *De Servo Arbitrio, On The Bondage of the Will*, in the

Founder's Library of Adonai College a few weeks ago. I have to admit that I was becoming rather bored with Luther's rantings against Erasmus, who after all was a terribly urbane sort of chap and was in so many ways the founder of modern scholarship; and in a spasm of vexation at the ignorant Luther's boorish dogmatism, I picked up the book and shook it violently.

'To my horror, the end papers at the back tore open. I hurriedly replaced the tome on the desk before anyone could even suspect that I had been abusing it.

'When the other two chaps in the Library disappeared through the door, I peeped under the back cover to see how much damage I had done. The crack was about five inches long. The Librarian, in the event that anyone should discover the tear, would probably think that it was due to the natural stresses and strains of repeatedly taking the volume off the shelf and putting it back again.

'I was just about to replace the book myself when I noticed a slip of paper poking through the tear.

'I glanced around. The place was quite empty, so I gently pulled the paper out of the binding. It was folded along its length twice. I unfolded it very carefully, for I quickly realised that although it had originally been very thick, it had become quite dry and brittle with age.

'What an extraordinary document it was! This is what it said:

'"A COMMINATION AGAINST YE DEVIL WORSHIPPERS OF EZEKIEL COLLEGE

'"Ye papists of Ezekiel House keep a devil in their college whom they worship. Yea, I have seen this with mine own eyes. God in His mercy preserve me from all contagion!

'"May the fires of Jehovah's wrath consume their hearts and bowels ..."

'And there was plenty more fulmination of that type.

'There was, however, no indication of who'd written the thing, or when, though I'd judge myself that it must have been a reformed clergyman of the time of Edward VI or perhaps the early years of Queen Elizabeth's reign.

'I didn't say anything to the Librarian, of course, because I was ashamed at having damaged the book. But my guilty conscience has insisted on summoning up the memory of the episode to rebuke me at regular intervals over the last few weeks. And then this bizarre letter arrives from Ezekiel like a thunderclap.'

Barnabas gazed at me with gleaming eyes.

'What are you going to do?' he asked.

'Visit Dr Potter, to be sure,' I replied.

***

Wednesday 4th October 1899

I consulted Crockford's clerical directory before setting off for Ezekiel.

Jerome Potter had read medicine at Oxford and then theology at Cuddesdon before setting off for Africa as both priest and doctor. It was evident, from his note to me, that he had been learning the ancient abjad in order to study Ethiopic texts, perhaps even the Garima Gospels, which some people, including the monks of Abuna Garima, believe to be as old as the Codex Sinaiticus, though I have to say that that seems very unlikely to me.

Potter had clearly not progressed very far with his studies, for had he done so he would surely have written to me in the language rather than merely transliterated English into its characters. To be sure, his deficiency in Ethiopic must have been due to his being a very busy man, for in addition to his work as a minister of the gospel, he had also taught tropical medicine at the Government College in Mombasa and, as Barnabas had mentioned, had acquired quite a formidable scientific reputation for investigating the typical diseases of the region. When I asked one of our King's medical men what he knew about Potter's work, he gave opinion that it would not be long before the man was elected a Fellow of the Royal Society.

From this, I concluded that Dr Potter was in all likelihood an earnest sort of chap, whom I should take seriously. Barney and I therefore trotted off to Ezekiel.

Now Ezekiel College is the second oldest college in the university. It was founded in 1289 by Jean de Beaujeu, Lord Bishop of Corpusty, a long abolished miniature diocese in a relatively obscure part of Norfolk, as his contribution to the Dominican revolution that was setting Europe alight with dogmatic fervour. The statutes of Ezekiel College require the teaching of the theological system of St Thomas Aquinas even to this day, three hundred or so years after the English Reformation; and the statutes are still obeyed, although the college is of course now quite Anglican in flavour, though with rather more than a mustard seed of Popery still. Indeed, since the rise of the Oxford Movement, it has been quite the fashion for Ezekiel men to convert to Rome.

I can never decide whether I like the place. It has an immensely distinguished reputation for historical scholarship in the medieval and modern periods, which is thoroughly deserved; but its dons display a commensurate smugness that I find rather vain and tiring. Architecturally, it has a lowering and block like solidity, which, no doubt, is due to the need to keep out the waters that periodically flood Coe Fen, where it sits, scowling enviously at its older neighbour, Peterhouse.

But it is like entering a dour castle - a dour Scottish castle on a gloomy rain sodden afternoon - rather than a place of enlightenment at that. Why is it, then, that Ezekiel's scholarly accomplishments are uniquely graceful and charming? I can only put this down to the cheerful limpidity of the Beaujolais wines that are customarily served at its High Table.

Barney and I entered the tunnel-like gatehouse, at the bottom of Little St Mary's Lane, and thrust our faces into the open window of the Porters' Lodge.

'Dr James and Mr Lamb, of King's College, to see Dr Potter,' I announced.

The porter on duty, a young man of gaunt and highly-strung appearance, with grey skin and glittering eyes, gazed at us uncertainly.

'Will you gen'lemen kindly wait a moment, while I fetches Mr Socks,' he said, and, before we had even the opportunity to query who the said Socks might be, slipped through a door into a back room.

A few moments later, the tense youth reappeared with an older man who, from his ruddy face and petty officer like manner, was evidently the Head Porter.

'What would your business be with Dr Potter, sir?' he enquired.

'That is a private matter,' I replied.

'It's just that the gentleman's very ill,' explained the Head Porter, calmly. 'And therefore I'm under orders to keep him secluded, to prevent any unnecessary strains and stresses, you see?'

'So I hear,' I replied, 'through the medium of mutual friends. I'm a fellow Ethiopic scholar of Dr Potter's, and I wish to see whether I can do anything for him.'

'You can't go burdening the doctor with work, sir.'

'We don't intend to. Merely to offer him such comfort as we can in his sickness.'

'Very well,' said the Head Porter, his eyes moving in a searching and rather hostile way from one to the other of us. 'You'll find him on B staircase, gentlemen. I'm sure he'll benefit from your conversation, but the Master's given strict instructions that Dr Potter's not to have any food or drink.'

'None at all?'

'Only what the Master himself prescribes, sir.'

'Oh, of course, your Master's a medical man himself, isn't he?'

'That he is, sir, and his instructions are to be strictly obeyed.'

Potter's rooms were right at the top of the stairs, which meant that Barnabas and I were nearly as devoid of breath as the unhealthy physician himself when we knocked on his oaken door and, after a decent pause of utter silence, entered his set.

Although the curtains were pulled back, the windows themselves were small - not much more than broadened slits, letting in very little of the scarce light that managed to enter the confines of Duns Scotus Court. A meagre fire was burning in the hearth in the centre of the wall opposite us, casting a low and flickering light over the books that lined the room. A desk, littered with papers and bottles of murky fluid, stood in front of the window. A sofa and two arm chairs had been pushed to the opposite end of the room, blocking a door that presumably led into Dr Potter's sleeping quarters. In their place stood a camp bed, on which lay the still but muttering form of the sick physician himself.

Potter knew who we were as soon as we loomed over his cot.

'James,' he whispered, his voice very hoarse, 'thank you for coming.'

'My dear fellow,' I replied, shocked. 'You look dreadful.'

The bedder's description was not inaccurate. What struck me the most as I gazed down on the poor man was how sunken his eyes were in their sockets. I felt as if I were looking down a well into scarcely visible water.

'I know of your interest in the arcane,' murmured poor Potter, his jaundiced and bloodshot eyes fixed on mine. I could see him wince as he saw them reflected in the lenses of my spectacles. 'I have read your account of the strange case of Mr Dennistoun and Canon Alberic's scrap book, and I hope that you can deliver me from the demon Belphegor, whose infernal fingers at this moment are probing and twisting my nerves and sinews, sir, pulling and stretching them beyond endurance.'

'But look here,' I replied. 'That stuff about Canon Alberic was a mere fiction, an invention of my own.'

'No, no, it was providence that led you to write the story; and led me to read it,' gasped Potter. 'I know also that you are well read in the arcane literature of the middle ages. You must be my exorcist.'

'What makes you think you are possessed?' enquired Barnabas.

A scurrying sound came from the grandfather clock and ran along the wainscot. Barney and I both heard it. We glanced at one another.

'Well?' I asked of Potter.

'I am commanded not to cast the Pearl before swine,' groaned Potter, 'but I must.'

'I beg your pardon?' replied Barney.

'I rather think Dr Potter is not referring to St Matthew 7:6,' I muttered.

'You will have not heard of the Pearl,' whispered Potter. 'It is the greatest treasure of this college, and is kept in the deepest and strongest of the Cellars of Ezekiel. I break the most solemn oath simply by telling you of its existence.'

'Surely, your greatest treasure is your incomparable collection of manuscripts?' I riposted. 'For Heaven's sake, you even possess a second century papyrus of Josephus's *Jewish War*!'

'That is but a dead thing,' laughed Potter, in a way that froze the marrow of my bones. 'The Pearl is alive, I tell you.'

'What on earth do you mean?' asked Barnabas.

'Oh, I will only put you fellows in mortal danger if I say more,' groaned Potter. 'How can I do that in all Christian conscience? Leiden, leiden, kreuz, kreuz, as the great Luther said; that is all.'

'We might be able to help you,' I suggested, 'the danger may in fact be less than you fear.'

'De profundis clamavi ad te, Domine, exaude vocem meam,' cried Dr Potter.

I could have sworn that at the moment Potter uttered the word 'Domine', two books parted in the bookshelf about twelve feet or so behind the sick man's bed. I looked up at the place, and saw the last moment of a sudden shift. Or at least, I thought I did. Skirting around the bottom of the cot, I walked over to the shelves and inspected the gap. There was a ventilation hole of some kind behind it, with a metal grille. The two books that had been pushed apart, though by what agency I could not imagine, were Gore's *Lux Mundi* and Parker's *Essays and Reviews*.

'What was that?' asked Barnabas.

'The books moved, I think.'

'No, not that. Didn't you hear it? An airy sound from over here, like a sharp intake of breath.'

My young friend was staring at the grandfather clock. I followed his gaze with my eyes.

'Good Lord,' I murmured. 'Look at the minute hand.'

The pointer was quivering, as if trying to advance while being forcibly held back.

'It is he,' cried Potter. 'It is he.'

'Who?' I asked.

I glanced at Barney and saw a flicker of fear cross his features.

'Roger,' gasped Potter. 'Roger of Ikenhoe.'

'And who, pray, is this Roger you speak of?'

A shriek of joy came into the room like a lance from the ventilation grille behind the book case. Potter opened his mouth to speak but could not. As his jaw worked up and down, I noticed his lips turn a pale blue, and a single blob of spittle fly off his tongue.

'What is going on?' asked Barnabas, in a fright.

'Morphia!' screamed Dr Potter, suddenly. 'I tried to kill him.'

'Whom?'

But Potter's teeth began to chatter uncontrollably. We could not get an answer from him.

'Someone is laughing on the stairs,' cried Barnabas. 'But it sounds like Potter's own laugh?'

I strode to the door and flung open the oak, but the staircase was, as I had expected it would be, quite empty.

***

A little later the same day

Dr Potter did seem to me to be ill and I wondered whether the best thing to do would be to leave and let the Master of Ezekiel get on with treating him. But, on the other hand, several features of the case made me feel uneasy.

For instance, I did not see how Potter could have created the physical movements and noises that we saw and heard whilst in his room.

'I feel as if we are being watched,' was Barney's comment on this.

Second, I had not liked the attitude of the men in the Porter's Lodge.

'Yes,' agreed Barnabas. 'It all feels very enclosed, doesn't it?'

'Is Potter at their mercy?' I wondered.

'What do you know of this Roger of Ikenhoe?' asked my young friend.

'Ikenhoe was St Botolph's monastery in the depths of Suffolk,' I replied, 'but I've never heard of this fellow Roger.'

'Was he a Fellow?'

'I didn't mean that, but by Heaven, you might be right.'

I scanned Potter's book shelves for anything that might bear on the history of Ezekiel College. After a minute or two, I noticed *The Registers of the House of the Prophet Ezekiel, in the Ancient University of Cambridge*, edited by Septimus Knapton DD, MDCCLXXXVII. Taking this down, I leafed through it until I found a chapter listing the names of all the Fellows since the foundation of the college.

'The name is clearly medieval,' I muttered, 'so if Roger's a Fellow, he should be in here.'

Potter began to groan again. His breathing sounded very hoarse.

'Water,' he moaned. 'Give me water.'

Barnabas looked for a jug of water but found only an empty one, quite dry.

'There's a drinking fountain in the court,' he said. 'I'll go and fill it.'

He left me turning the pages of the *Registers*.

He had not been gone for more than a minute when I found a line or two on Roger. This is what the book said:

Roger of Ikenhoe. Admitted as Fellow 1292. Member of the Order of Preachers (St Dominic) attached to St Botolph's Abbey. Author of Commentary on Aquinas's *Summa Contra Gentiles*. Author of unfinished *Historia Albigensium Haeresis*. Killed by the heretic Hugo (nephew of Peter) Waldo, at St Bertrand de Comminges, 1296. Body miraculously preserved from corruption, brought back to England & buried in Ezekiel's chapel.

I whistled at this. St Bertrand de Comminges! No wonder poor old Potter had fixed upon me to help rid him of his delusions - if that is what they were.

Barney returned at this point, a jug filled to the brim in his hand.

'You'll never believe this,' he cried, 'but that waxen-faced young porter tried to confiscate my jug!'

'What?' I laughed. 'Surely they don't think it's interfering of us to give the poor soul some water!'

'He seemed to,' replied Barnabas, taking a glass off Potter's desk and pouring some water into it. He went over to the patient and gave the poor chap a few sips to drink while I read out what I'd found in Knapton's *Registers*.

Then Potter tried to speak but could only whisper.

'What's he saying?' I asked.

Barnabas put his ear to the man's lips.

'I tried to kill him,' Barnabas repeated. 'Morphia. But it only enraged Belphegor. I want to save him but I'm scared. "For that which I do I allow not: for what I would, that I do not; but what I hate, that I do."'

'Kill whom?' I asked. 'Surely not ...'

'I don't know. Who is Belphegor?'

Potter emitted a strangulated scream.

'The German bishop Petrus Binsfeldius in the sixteenth century held him to be the demon of sloth,' I said. 'More recent and more reliable scholars suppose that he derives from the Moabite god בַּעַל-פְּעוֹר (or in plain English, Baal-Peors) by whom the people of Israel were led astray in the city of Shittim. Binsfeldius claimed that Belphegor seduced lazy people with inventions and discoveries that would quickly and easily make them rich and famous.'

'Save us both,' croaked Potter. 'The grave. The cellars.'

And then he suffered some kind of fit.

***

Later still

Back in my own rooms on D staircase in King's, I lighted a pipe full of Sobranie and sat back in my chair.

'My dear Barnabas,' I opined. 'Rather a gruesome interview, that. There's something devilish in it.'

'Indeed.'

'I fear that we must simply step back and watch this battle from afar, lest we ourselves be drawn into it.'

'But I'm a clergyman, Monty, I can't do that.'

'Oh dear, oh dear. You take too high a view of your vocation, my boy.'

'You make me sound like a Stylite!'

'Hmm. I'm not sure that even the top of a pillar would offer sanctuary in a case like this.'

'A case like this? A case of what?'

'I hardly dare utter the words in question.'

'Oh, come, come, Monty. This is 1899!'

'You mean this is more a matter for an alienist than an exorcist?'

'Of course. Poor old Dr Potter needs better medical attention than he seems to be getting from the Master of Ezekiel.'

'But if that is what you think, why do you feel that you have a particular duty as a clergyman?'

'His mania is clearly of a religious character. He might be willing to listen to words of hope and comfort from me. Don't you think?'

'I really don't know.'

'Well, I'm going back there later to converse with the poor fellow again.'

'Then I must assist you with the requisite facts. As you know, I catalogued the manuscripts of Ezekiel College last year. Among them was a report from Christopher Wren to Dr John Brother, the then Master, from the year 1664, about the planned restoration of the college chapel to its catholic glories following the demise of the Commonwealth. The Master wished to beautify the chapel with a new high altar, ornately carved stalls, beautiful stained glass and a fine organ with three manuals and pedals. But Wren took the view that the current organ loft was unsafe for so enlarged an instrument, and decided that he must build a new one with stronger foundations. That involved excavating the ground under the loft, which is where the grave of Robert of Ikenhoe is located, alongside those of several other former Fellows. When Wren went to exhume Robert's body, in order to sink a central pier into the ground, he found that the grave was quite empty. There was no evidence, he said, of any body having been buried there, though the graves on either side did indeed contain what little was left of corpses from in all likelihood the late middle ages.'

'So where are Roger of Ikenhoe's remains, Monty?'

'They may simply have perished, of course. But it is striking, is it not, that while the grave is reported to be empty, our friend Dr Potter appears to be obsessed by the man who is meant to be buried there.'

'Do you think that Potter has somehow discovered the real grave?'

'That might account for why he feels troubled by Roger of Ikenhoe's spirit, and in need of exorcism,' I admitted.

'Perhaps he has taken something of historic value from the grave, and is troubled by guilt? Perhaps he took this pearl that he mentioned?'

'I suppose that's possible.'

'I wonder where the grave is?'

'I should hazard that if one exists at all, it will be in the Mausoleum of the Masters.'

'The Mausoleum of the Masters? I've never heard of such a place.'

'Really? It's quite well known. The Mausoleum is in the famous Cellars of Ezekiel, which stand underneath the whole of the college apart from the chapel. Tradition has it that every Master has to agree to being eventually entombed in the Cellars as a precondition of his being elected to the magisterial seat. In more recent days, this has proven to be quite controversial with the families of the distinguished gentlemen nowadays elected as Master, for they forfeit all the usual rights of the bereaved and may only visit the tombs of their loved ones when permitted to do so by the Inner Court of the college.'

'The Inner Court?'

'A sort of supreme council consisting of the Master, the Dean and the Bursar, with the Head Porter as its ancient Constable. It's said to take all the really important decisions at Ezekiel.'

'So, they wouldn't let us into this Mausoleum?'

'I rather doubt it, my dear Barnabas.'

'But we might find the genesis of Dr Potter's obsession if we go down there and look around a bit.'

I hesitated to respond to this assertion, for I knew that Barney would seize upon what I should say.

'Well,' I ventured, 'I happen to know from an old friend of mine at Peterhouse, that there is an air vent from the Cellars of Ezekiel that happens to open into the Scholars' Garden at the southern extremity of his college. There was a dispute some years ago between Ezekiel and Peterhouse about the exact line of the boundary wall when the ancient masonry suddenly crumbled, and Peterhouse rebuilt the wall over the top of the air vent - but incorporated the aperture into the wall. There is a metal grille, to be sure, but I also happen to know from my walks with my Petrean friend Dodsworth that the grille is loose.'

'So, we can get in by crawling through this vent?'

'Only if we have not habitually committed the sin of gluttony. And don't mind being scratched to blazes by the rose bushes that obscure it from public view.'

***

Thursday 5th October 1899

We went in late that night.

I had to take off my jacket and waistcoat to wriggle in, but Barney had no trouble at all. The drop from the vent to the floor must have been about ten feet, but we descended like rock climbers, using the courses of the stonework to take our weight. This was tough on my fingers, but necessary.

We took a couple of small lanterns with us and a box of matches, and of course, I carried a notebook and several pencils as I usually do.

We found ourselves in a flagged corridor with sturdy walls and a stone vault overhead. This ran away into darkness to our right and left, that is, along a north-south axis. Behind us was the base of the boundary wall, and in front of us an internal wall with doorways that appeared to give access to store rooms. We looked in a couple - they were not locked - and found old garden furniture and, bizzarely, a stuffed bear.

'The Mausoleum is near the chapel,' I whispered to Barney, as we were staring into one of these rooms, 'which is on this side of Ezekiel, but to our right. I know that a staircase leads down to the Mausoleum from the Ante-Chapel.'

'So, we should head northwards?'

'Yes.'

We did this but came to a blank. A stone wall stopped the passage completely.

'Let's see if the opposite way leads to the chapel stairs,' I suggested.

This proved correct. We walked southwards, then did a right-angle turn to the west, and then found that the tunnel branched. The passage we were in continued straight ahead, but another one, of exactly the same dimensions, went off to the right.

We took the tunnel that we knew would lead us towards the chapel. After a minute, we found ourselves in a vaulted square. A flight of steps descended to our level in the centre of the right-hand side of this square. Opposite it, another tunnel led into the heart of the college.

'Down there, I should judge, is the Mausoleum,' I whispered to Barney. 'Right under the Great Hall.'

'You don't mean to say they sit down at table over the magisterial corpses?'

'Those dead men are the founders of the feast,' I replied, with a smile.

I shone my lantern down that tunnel and set off.

After perhaps another minute, we found ourselves in a circular arcade. I say arcade, but this was true of only one side of the tunnel. The other was a solid unbroken wall. The arcade side, however, had, under each arch, a statue of a former Master of Ezekiel. I found it utterly fascinating to see the stylistic change from the simple limestone figures of pious thirteenth century monks to worm-ridden transi figures of the late fourteenth century to polished marble images of princes of the church of the late seventeenth century, where the influence of Bernini's interest in dramatic psychology was quite evident.

I was absorbed in studying these remarkable pieces and thinking of Tertullian's dictum - Respice post te, mortalem te esse memento - when I heard Barnabas call me.

'Monty, come and look at this,' he urged.

He was pointing at a smooth stone inset among the rough blocks of the solid circular wall that formed the inner circle of the arcade. I held up my lantern and saw lettering.

ITERUM SIMILE EST REGNUM CAELORUM HOMINI NEGOTIATORI QUARENTI BONAS MARGARITAS : INVENTA AUTEM UNA PRETIOSA MARGARITA ABIIT ET VENDEDIT OMNIA QUAE HABUIT ET EMIT EAM

'Matthew, Chapter 13, verses 45 and 46, in the Vulgate,' said Barney.

'Again, the kingdom of heaven is like unto a merchant man, seeking goodly pearls: Who, when he had found one pearl of great price, went and sold all that he had and bought it,' I murmured.

'What do you think is behind this wall?' asked Barney.

I shrugged my shoulders. 'A pearl of great price?'

'Come on, let's walk around it,' said my young friend; and he trotted off, his lantern held up to look for a door into the inner circus.

We found no entrance, but roughly opposite the Latin inscription, on a diametrical line, we found a Greek one. It was of the same text. I should judge that it came from the Codex Vaticanus.

Πάλιν ὁμοία ἐστὶν ἡ βασιλεία τῶν οὐρανῶν ἀνθρώπῳ ἐμπόρῳ ζητοῦντι καλοὺς μαργαρίτας : εὑρὼν δὲ ἕνα πολύτιμον μαργαρίτην ἀπελθὼν πέπρακεν πάντα ὅσα εἶχεν καὶ ἠγόρασεν αὐτόν

'Interesting,' I remarked. 'The placing of the texts suggests that this axis is important somehow, but for the life of me I can't see why.'

We completed our circumambulation but could find no means of ingress to the core.

'Let's read the inscriptions again,' said Barnabas, 'and see if they conceal any clues. I'll go and look at the Greek, you read the Latin. Read it carefully, Monty, and see if you can spot any clues.'

'Or hear them,' I remarked. 'I'll read mine aloud. That will help me to be accurate.'

'Good idea,' said Barney, and he disappeared into the darkness with his small light.

I stood in front of the Vulgate and stared at it for several moments, looking for any irregularities in the inscription. I could detect none. Then I began to recite the text in a sibilant whisper.

From above me, I could hear a slight echo of Barnabas quoting the Greek at the other side of the rotunda. It must have been bouncing around the vault and reaching me rather diminished.

We finished our speech. Silence settled again and I was beginning to suppose that we had been wasting our time when I heard a grating noise. I was alarmed by this as I thought it might betoken the arrival of some college authority, so I quickly made my way in the clockwise direction, expecting to find Barnabas seeking me anticlockwise.

I did find Barnabas but he was stationary and staring into a doorway that had opened, of its own accord, it seemed, in the inner circle. This was exactly halfway between the two inscriptions, at the southernmost point of the inner wall.

'It's an iron door with just a veneer of chiselled stone,' he remarked. 'There is no handle or bolt on the outside, only these on the inside - look.'

He held his lantern up to show me two bolts, one at the top, the other at the bottom.

'How devious,' I remarked. 'But what's inside?'

It was utterly dark in there. We could see no further than a yard into the chamber.

'I don't know. Shall we go in?'

'Of course. This is far too interesting to ignore.'

We stepped, though not without anxiety, into the gloom.

***

At first we could see nothing. Instinctively keeping close together, we tried to exponentiate the light of our lamps; but the figure of eight that we cast ahead of us illuminated only the cold flagstones of the floor.

'Am I deceived,' whispered Barney, 'or is the interior of this chamber larger than its exterior?'

'It's merely an illusion of the darkness,' I replied.

We made our way to what we felt should be the centre of the crypt, which is where we instinctively felt that the focus of our interest should be, but had no way of checking whether our bearing was correct. We knew we had gone wrong when we reached another stone wall and had still found nothing. So we turned round and set off on a slightly different bearing.

I was astonished when we once again reached a curving wall without encountering anything other than dust on the ground.

'Maybe the place is empty, like Potter's ravings,' suggested Barney.

'One more try,' I counselled.

So we set off again on a different bearing for our third attempt at finding the room's contents.

We had taken perhaps two dozen steps, and had both begun to sigh with disappointment, when of a sudden a man stepped into the light of our lamps from beside us.

'Good Lord!' ejaculated Barney. The man must have been by his side.

I fixed my eyes on the face of the new fellow.

It was the visage of a man in perhaps his middle thirties, but one of which the skin looked thin and grey and lined with too much experience. The mouth was straight and unsmiling, the lips giving just a pale hint of pink. In the eyes, I could see only the blackness of the pupils. There was a flickering of the right eyelid. A thin and patchy black beard covered the cheeks and chin. The man raised a trembling right hand to shade his eyes from the light, and I noticed that he was wearing the white tunic and black cappa and hood of a Dominican. The strange man's mouth began to move as he stepped stepped back to the very edge of visibility.

'Eftsoone,' he murmured, 'the kyngdom of heuenes is lijk to a marchaunt, that sechith good margaritis; but whanne he hath foundun o precious margarite, he wente, and selde alle thingis that he hadde, and bouyte it.'

The words were accompanied by a foul stench, as of a man whose mouth and lungs were full of dark rottenness. Both Barnabas and I stepped back involuntarily.

'I haue ye seen bifor this tyme,' stated the Dominican.

'Who are you?' asked Barnabas.

The Dominican sighed heavily. The stench made Barney take a handkerchief from his pocket and clasp it over his nose and mouth.

'What are you doing here, my friend?' I asked.

'The vanyte of vanytees' said the Dominican, 'the vanyte of vanytees, and alle thingis ben vanite. What hath a man more of alle his trauel, bi which he traueilith vndur the sunne? Generacioun passith awei, and generacioun cometh; but the erthe stondith with outen ende.'

'You are Roger of Ikenhoe?' asked Barney.

The Dominican nodded.

'Y am very heuyed, my Cristens,' said the Dominican. 'Y am constreyneden bi the Maisters and my deuel to witness thingis that may not be teld, and then telle of tho - efte tyme and tyme.'

'How do you come to be here?' demanded Barnabas.

'Bi curse of Hugo Waldo,' replied the Dominican. 'A double heretik, a Waldense but also a louer of wickid thingis tauyt of Cathars bi that false Franciscain, Bernard Delicieux.'

Now, really, this seemed too good to be true to me. The chap before us was probably an incontinent lunatic who had been locked in the cellar by the Master and Fellows because of his unbearable stench. I resolved to put him to the test by a snippet of new knowledge that I had discovered only recently and had not yet published.

'Are you familiar with the *Ambigua* of St Maximus the Confessor?' I asked.

'Maximos, certes,' replied the Dominican. 'My ordre is halewid to lernyng.'

'In particular,' I continued, 'are you familiar with the Latin translation made from a Syriac version, by a Dominican called Edward of Epping, made about 1280?'

'Certes.'

'Splendid. Tell me, how does it differ from the one made by Eriugena in the ninth century?'

'Princeps,' said the Dominican, 'it hath a thridde sette of Ambigua for Basil, Presbyter of Tsageri, as well as they to Bishop Johannes and Abbot Thomas.'

My mouth fell open.

Barney saw this and shuddered.

'There is so much you could tell me,' I murmured to the Dominican.

'Y woot so.'

He turned away from me slightly.

I noticed Barney putting a handkerchief over his nose and mouth.

'Take the Gospel of Thomas,' I cried to the Dominican. 'You have read it?'

'Naturaliter' said he.

'How many Latin versions are there?'

'Oh, many. These thingis be trivia, mi Cristen.'

'And how do these versions describe the will of the Father at the end of the Gospel?'

'I can't stand the stench in here for much longer,' said Barney.

'My dear Barnabas, I have an opportunity here to remedy the corruption of the Vienna palimpsest!'

'Let's get out of here, Monty.'

'Do you have a pipe with you?' I asked.

'Yes.'

I took my tobacco pouch from my pocket and thrust it into his hand.

'Then here,' I said, 'smoke some of my Balkan Sobranie - it's highly aromatic - it should drive away the obnoxious odours.'

'Well?' I demanded of the Dominican, while Barnabas lighted his pipe.

The Dominican opened his mouth to answer my question, but suddenly screamed in some unintelligible and high-pitched inhuman tongue, while - I know not how - smiling sweetly at the same time.

As the smoke from Barney's pipe formed a dense cloud around us, swirling in the light of our lanterns, the Dominican stepped into it and breathed in lungs full of smoke eagerly.

The fellow just disintegrated into a million flakes of - well - dandruff, which floated in the light like so much snow around a street lamp on a still evening, before settling onto the flags of the floor.

***

Thus did Ezekiel College lose its Pearl.

What a loss! No more easy scholarship for the Ezekelians.

Barney and I, unnerved by the whole business, just ran for the air vent into Peterhouse's garden. We clambered, with scant dignity, up the stone wall and squeezed out into the scented air.

Fortunately, my old friend Dodsworth of Peterhouse, a lamentable Graecist but an excellent judge of port, had lent me his keys for the night, so Barnabas and I were able to make our way through the Deer Park, across Old Court and out by the back gate into Little St Mary's Lane, without being detected by the night porter.

Back in my rooms at King's, we medicated our nerves with liberal doses of brandy.

'What about Dr Potter?' asked Barney. 'Do you think this will have cured him?'

I gazed in surprise at my young friend.

'I rather fear not,' I said.

'So, we need to help him still?'

I paused.

'Sometimes,' I said, cautiously, 'we have to accept that we are quite powerless to help another. Our best policy, my dear fellow, is to give Ezekiel as wide a berth as possible. That is certainly what I intend to do.'

'But how can you say that, Monty? Surely, it's our Christian duty to help Potter?'

'I think you'll find that we've merely made things worse for him.'

I saw the vexation mounting in my young friend's face.

'Let's leave that discussion for daylight,' I said. 'I think we both need to sleep now.'

***

Friday 6th October 1899

This morning I slept late and was woken by someone thumping relentlessly on my outer door.

I rose and clad myself in my woollen dressing gown.

My bedmaker had evidently been in already, for someone had cleaned the brandy glasses and restored them to their place in my cupboard. A new fire was burning in the grate too.

I opened the oak.

Barney stood on the landing, accompanied by two sturdy ladies.

'Monty,' cried Barnabas, his eyes gleaming, 'Mrs Frior and Mrs Gull are here with some startling news.'

'Really? But I'm not dressed for receiving visitors,' I remarked, coldly. 'Especially ladies.'

'You'll want to hear this,' insisted Barney, who seemed dangerously excited to me.

'It's poor Dr Potter,' broke in Mrs Frior. 'He's dead, your Directorship, sir.'

I was astonished that Mrs Frior knew of my post at the Fitzwilliam Museum.

'Dead?'

'I found him myself this morning, sir, a-lying on the floor, a needle sticking into his left arm like a flag pole it was.'

'Good heavens.'

'Oh, his face, it wor all screwed up,' continued Mrs Frior. 'Hanguish, that's what he felt as he died, if I'm not an 'onest woman.'

'It's a scandal,' broke in Mrs Gull. 'He took 'is own life.'

'I think you might be jumping to conclusions there, Mrs G,' counselled Barney.

'There's damnation waiting for them as what takes their own life,' insisted the indignant bedder.

'At what time did he pass away?' I enquired.

'The Master saw to him,' answered Mrs Frior. 'And he reckoned it must a' been in the small hours.'

'You said the Master seemed preoccupied?' prompted Barney.

'Yes, your Reverence. The 'Ead Porter kept coming to him, saying that he'd searched everywhere, but couldn't find him.'

'Find who?'

'I don't know, sir. But Mr Cox, the 'Ead Porter, kept saying that 'e reckoned "it" 'ad gone for good.'

'I see.'

'It'd be the end o' the college, the Master said. I don't know why.'

'It all sounds a lamentable business,' I remarked. 'Where is is Dr Potter's corpse now?'

'Oh, I don't know, sir. Mr Cox was asked to fetch the undertaker. They may 'a taken him by now.'

I gazed at Barnabas. 'You recall our final conversation last night?'

He nodded.

'I was right, you see.'

'He was very ill,' broke in Mrs Frior. 'I'm sure you gen'lemen did your best for 'im.'

Of course, I couldn't say anything to the bedder, or to Barney for that matter, but I rather think that in the circumstances, poor old Potter did his best for himself. He had made, in my view, his own strange 'beakerful of the warm south'.

***

Wednesday 11th October 1899

I've just got back from Potter's funeral at the Ascension Burial Ground. A most extraordinary thing has happened. The service had finished and I was standing in All Souls Lane chatting to the clergyman from Ezekiel when the two gravediggers rushed out into the road and grabbed hold of us.

"E's gone,' cried the lankier of the two fellows.

'Under our very noses,' complained the other.

'There ain't no trace of 'im.'

'What on earth are you talking about?' asked the chaplain.

'Come an' look!' said the tall one.

We followed them back to the open grave.

The coffin stood on its end, with the head at the bottom of the grave. The lid had been forced off, for it was splintered in a few places. The thing was quite empty. I looked around for the corpse, but it was not visible anywhere.

'Where's the body?' I asked.

The sextons shrugged. They looked genuinely mystified.

The chaplain was severe. 'How did this happen?'

'We wos keepin' our distance from the mourners,' protested the diggers.

'You left the coffin unattended?'

'Only fer a minute or two.'

'So as nobody would hear us as we started to shovel the soil back, like.'

'We wos behind that bush o'er there.'

'Didn't 'ear a thing. Just found the box bashed open when we came back with our spades.'

It had been raining lightly for most of the day and the ground was damp round about. The matting around the grave prevented any tracks from being visible, and neither could I find any on the nearby grass; but a little further away, where the grass gave way to a soil-fringed gravel path, I could see some faint prints in the soft earth.

Just one pair of feet, I'd say.

***

Thursday 12th October 1899

I could tell, as we sipped port after dinner, and chatted inconsequentially about the travels of John Moschus, that Barney was anxious to tell me something - but also not a little afraid to do so.

'Well,' I said at last, putting down my glass. 'What ails thee, priest-at-arms?'

My friend grimaced, but spoke.

'Last night, as I was reading *Martin Chuzzlewit* and chuckling at the verbal habits of Mrs Gamp, I heard a scratching at my door. It must have been about eleven-thirty. I rose from my seat and moved over to the door. The oak was open, by the way. Certainly, the sound I heard put me in mind of someone fumbling for the handle. I listened carefully. I could hear no whispering, or even breathing for that matter. Of a sudden, I pulled open the door; but the landing was quite empty.'

'Mice, surely?'

'Maybe.'

'You seem unconvinced.'

'There was a terrible smell of wet rot that hadn't been there before.'

'You should speak to the bursar about getting your staircase redecorated.'

'Perhaps.'

'How are your mathematics coming along?'

Barney was, in addition to being a clergyman with a respectable command of Greek, a wrangler of no small distinction. He was, I knew, writing a paper on the speed of light.

'Oh, pretty well. Poincaré is quite right that the laws of nature can be written in their simplest form when the velocity of light is treated as a constant. I'm sure there's huge potential in combining that insight with Hendrik Lorentz's notions of local time and length contraction, but I'm not making much progress on finding the equations for the electrodynamics at present.'

I placed my hand on my friend's arm.

'Don't worry,' I said. 'You've been distracted. I'm sure you'll soon be under way again.'

Barney smiled, a little doubtfully.

***

Tuesday 24th October 1899

I've noticed that Barnabas has started to take holy communion every day. His practice ever since I've known him has hitherto been to attend only twice a week.

What's more, I called round at his rooms today. I knocked sharply and, without waiting for answer, just walked in. I caught him in the middle of raising the eucharistic host in his own private service.

He flushed but thrust the wafer into his mouth and, I should judge, swallowed it virtually whole.

'Come back later, Monty,' he pleaded.

'Are you ill?' I asked.

'I'm fine,' he said. 'I just need building up.'

I stared at him.

'Spiritually.'

I nodded and shewed myself out.

***

Wednesday 25th October 1899

It's been over two weeks since Potter's funeral, and the poor fellow's body has still not been found.

The Dean, it seems, was commending my young friend for his remarkable devotion to the eucharist, and gently enquiring whether he was - perhaps - 'suffering from doubt', when Barney suddenly flamed up and declared that 'the whole thing' was 'utterly useless anyway'.

Barney stormed into my study just after chapel yesterday morning, picked up my tobacco jar, and strode off with it. I could scarcely concentrate on *The Times* after that. When, after an hour or two, I went around to his rooms to reclaim my property, I found that he'd already smoked half of what had been in the jar.

'I can only thank you, Monty,' he muttered, sullenly. 'I must go and buy some more.'

He insists that he can smoke nothing other than Balkan Sobranie.

***

Thursday 2nd November 1899

Barney has become a compulsive smoker. At least, I never see him without a burning pipe in his mouth; and I'm not the only chap to have said this.

***

Friday 3rd November 1899

I was reading Gairdner's edition of the *Paston Letters* today, and wondering what light they might throw on Shakespeare's inspiration for his great character Falstaff, when I heard the sound of a woman screaming below my window.

Disturbed by the thought that I might have attracted a hysterical female admirer, I went and looked down into Front Court to see if the lady in question was passably beautiful.

But the distressed gentlewoman was pointing up towards the pinnacles of the chapel.

My eyes followed the line indicated by the lady's arm.

How astonished I was to see my poor friend Barnabas clinging to the taper of the sixth pinnacle from the western end of the chapel roof. I could tell it was he from his profuse blonde hair. He was looking down at the ground longingly, and then back along the roof; repeatedly. I quickly realised that a diabolical temptation was passing through his mind.

Then I thought I noticed why. An indistinct figure was crawling towards Barney, from the south-western turret, partly obscured by the embattled stone screen along the edge of the roof. There was something about this black clothed figure that was unpleasantly grey and green, and I must confess that I began to feel quite queasy.

The Head Porter appeared by the turret and ran along the roof towards Barney. Distracted by the vigour of this old and admirable college servant, I lost sight of the crawling figure. When I searched the scene with my eyes for the strange form again, I could not see it at all.

Mr Blair, the Head Porter, seized hold of Barney, and pulled him down from the pinnacle.

The lady below ceased to scream, mercifully.

***

Tuesday 7th November 1899

I didn't really want to but I went to see Barnabas today. He'd been asking for me, apparently.

I found him febrile in bed. Trembling visibly. He'd evidently been trying to work, for he was surrounded by sheets of paper on which he'd written down formulae and equations that made no sense to me.

'Light,' he said, as I took his hand. 'All information is carried by light.'

'And darkness?' I enquired.

'The absence of light is itself information.'

'Are you making progress on your paper?'

He shook his head.

'There is a contradiction,' he muttered. 'I can't rid myself of it.'

'Can I get you anything?'

'Wine,' he said. 'Red wine. The Dean won't give me any.'

I did not care to ask what use he would make of the wine.

'Very well,' I said.

'Listen to the wind,' gasped my decaying friend.

'I can scarcely hear it.'

'It keens so. Drives me crazy. Don't go, Monty. Stay with me, won't you?'

***

I saw Mrs Gull on the stairs.

'I'm very disappointed in Mr Lamb,' she cried, squeezing her broom as if she wished to throttle it.

'He's unwell,' I murmured.

'He's wicked,' she protested.

'Why?'

'He's succumbed to the drink!'

She leaned forward and tapped me on the chest, which I thought was rather Radical of her.

'I'm a broad-minded woman,' she continued, 'even though I'm tee-total myself; but I can't not protest when I see a fine man like that destroying his soul and body through strong liquor. It isn't right, Doctor James, it just isn't, is it?'

This gave me an idea. In addition to the red wine, I'd send Barnabas a bottle of brandy every now and then. After all, the poor fellow needs all the consolation he can get.

***

Monday 13th November 1899

Barnabas Lamb has finally been expelled from King's. His fatal offence was to wander into the chapel, quite completely drunk, during Evensong, shouting about 'that bloody trumpet'.

'Incorruptible my foot!' he shrieked, as the Head Porter dragged him away.

Lamb tried to bite the man's hand.

Naturally, the Dean could stand no more of this nonsense, and he dismissed Mr Lamb from his post as Vice-Chaplain with immediate effect. The Council ratified the decision when Lamb appealed.

I am feeling a little guilty about the whole business, I must admit, so I gave Lamb £100 and advised him to sail to India and seek out the wisdom of the East.

He took my money without a word of thanks - in fact, without a word of any kind - and left.

***

Friday 12th January 1900

I have just had a telegram from the District Collector in Kangra in the Punjab telling me that Barnabas Lamb has been found dead. My name and address was scrawled on a piece of paper in his trouser pocket as his next of kin, it seems. Quite absurdly.

***

Friday 9th March 1900

Today a long letter arrived from the District Collector in Kangra.

I will summarise the main points:

It seems that Barney Lamb earned a little money by teaching mathematics to the natives.

He rented a room in the house of the widow of a retired army officer in Dharamshala. One evening in January, the widow, Mrs Baxter, gave Lamb an extra bucket of coal as snow was starting to fall outside, and noticed as she did so that Lamb had already been drinking quite heavily. His speech was slurred. She quite distinctly heard Lamb, who occupied a room in the basement of the house, lock his door behind him as she climbed back upstairs.

During the night, the landlady dreamed that two tomcats were fighting beneath her bed. She woke up but all was quiet; so she fell asleep again quickly. At dawn, she again awakened, and this time thought that she could smell breakfast being prepared. This surprised her, so she climbed out of bed to check what the servants were doing. When she opened her door, she was shocked by the acrid smell of burned meat. Following the trail of the smell on the air, she found herself at Lamb's door. She knocked but there was no answer. She banged harder. The servants, disturbed by the sound, appeared. She ordered a strong man to break down the door.

Inside Lamb's room, they found two pairs of legs protruding from the hearth. One pair she recognised as Lamb's, from the clothes. The other, she said, was dressed in the tattered remains of trousers, and the skin was covered in green mould. In the fireplace itself was a heap of warm ash, and several scorched bones. She was surprised, apparently, that there were so few bones. Evidently a hardy woman.

The police inspector found my name and address on a scrap of paper in a pocket of the better pair of trousers. In the other pair he found a piece of paper, on which was a strange script he could not recognise. The District Collector, knowing of my renown as a scholar, has taken the liberty of sending it to me for my inspection.

It is in Ethiopic, and spells out the name 'Belphegor'.

I wonder if I should strengthen the locks on my doors?

And windows?

THE HEARTIES OF ADONAI

Thursday 12th February 1903

Oh, dear. I fell asleep in my armchair while reading Greek Text A of the Infancy Gospel of Thomas, and the damnable book gave me a terrible dream. It paints the boy Jesus as being, quite frankly, wicked. I fail to see how the nasty actions ascribed to him in it could have been seen as laudable in any generation!

For instance, Jesus, by a sharp word, completely withered up the son of Annas the scribe, merely because the latter had drained away a puddle of water that Jesus had made with walls of mud. Later, the young Christ struck another child dead just for bumping into his shoulder while running through the village. Then our Lord went on to scold and humiliate the old scholar Zacchaeus for presuming to teach him the Greek language - which Jesus, being divine, already knew perfectly well, of course.

Thank goodness, I am not a theologian! But I do dream, and the Infancy Gospel gave me a dreadful nightmare. I was at Evensong in chapel, and the choristers, as they sang the psalms antiphonally, began to wage vocal war on one another, the north stalls against the south, and the south against the north. By some occult power of telekinesis, the boys hurled prayer books, lighted candles, musical scores, bottles of cough medicine, bags of sweets, pocket watches, spectacles and hassocks at one another over the head of the master of choristers. Oh, my soul, how the beauty and solemnity of Evensong was utterly ruined! And a great wailing soared up to the stones of the vaulted roof from both sets of stalls, as choirboys' hair burst into yellow flame, eyes turned black-blue, and lips bled holly berry red.

This is what comes of reading the Apocrypha in one's arm chair of an afternoon.

One wonders at how religious sensibilities vary so much from one devotee to another over time and space. I suppose a chap should be thankful that in the steady unfolding of time, Providence has blessed us, here in England, with the good sense and decorum of the Anglican Church – truly, a light to lighten the Scots, the French, the Hibernians and all the rest of those rum foreign types.

But enough of my dream. I must remember tomorrow to look up the times of trains to Stamboul as I remain keen to see if I can track down the manuscript of Hegesippus' *Five Commentaries on the Acts of the Church*, circa AD 170, which, or so Zahn and Förster have argued, still exists in a collection in the town of Rodosto near Constantinople. Oh, I know there was a fire, which is said to have destroyed most of the library there; but would it not be worth the effort to see if Hegesippus is indeed the one surviving manuscript from the blaze? Think how much it would tell us about the Church of Jerusalem in the years immediately after the death and resurrection of Jesus Christ, under the episcopal government of James, his rather Pharisaic brother. But I must first resolutely put aside all my doubts about venturing into the empire of Johnny Turk.

***

I had barely put down my pen from writing the above about Hegesippus, when there sounded forth a very determined knock on my door.

'Come in,' I called.

The whited oak gaped and revealed Edmund Pedigree, a Fellow of Adonai College and one of those natural science types who spend hours and hours in the Cavendish

Laboratory making sparks and electrical waves and talking incessantly about plum puddings. Pedigree is a huge chap with a huge moustache, and broad shouldered, and he occluded the light from the staircase just as effectively as the door does itself. He used to row for his college, and has a couple of Blues, I think, and is now Senior Treasurer of the Adonai Boat Club. I don't know him very well, but his brother, Alfred, a remarkable botanist, is a great friend of mine here at King's.

'Hullo, Monty,' said Edmund, twirling his soft hat in his hands.

'This is a rare honour,' I replied. 'Do come in, my dear fellow. Tea? Crumpets?'

'Well, only if you were going to make some anyway.'

'Oh, indubitably,' I said, inspecting my watch. 'Exactly the right time.'

I put fresh coal on the fire, and my kettle on the gas ring.

'I'm sorry to turn up unannounced,' said Edmund, while I prepared the refreshments, 'but I'm afraid I really do need to consult you about a most bizarre business at my college.'

'Oh, really? What's that?'

'You haven't heard?'

'About what?'

'About one of our young men.'

'Really, you need to be more specific, I think.'

'Of course. Well, I'm talking about Eustace Blythe.'

'Never heard of him.'

'He's dead.'

'I'm sorry to hear that. But what has the unfortunate Mr Blythe to do with me?'

'Look here, you're famous for your interest in the occult, Monty, and the manner of young Blythe's death is … well, far from normal.'

'I'm just too busy to get involved, Edmund.'

'But it really is the most puzzling business, old man. Eustace was a young chap of the soundest health. He rowed bow in our First VIII, and very efficiently too, a master of technique with the blade. But earlier today, he was found murdered in his rooms.'

'Oh, I say, that's ghastly.'

'Ghastlier than you can imagine. His body is quite intact externally. There's not the slightest disturbance to his skin. But he's as dead as a stone; and beside the corpse there was a … a neat mound of …'

'Of what? Come on, out with it.'

'Of blood vessels.'

'What?'

Edmund rolled his eyes.

'You won't believe this, Monty, but the chap's entire circulatory system had been removed from his body and left there, beside him on the rug. Without making the slightest mark on the body, or shedding any blood – or at least, not externally.'

I was tempted to laugh, but Edmund looked genuinely shocked, quite grave.

'How do you know it was *his* circulatory system that was on the carpet?'

'Because the pathologist, on opening him up, found it missing from his corpse; and the cavities of the body were filled with the blood that should have been in the veins and arteries.'

'Good Lord!'

'You can say that again! The medics are at a loss to say how this could have happened.'

'So, you think this is a supernatural business?'

'I'm a natural scientist, Monty. All I can say is - it seems quite unnatural to me.'

'Tell me the broader circumstances.'

'Blythe lived in a set of rooms at the top of B staircase in Old Court. The man in the set opposite, Carruthers, was holding a champagne and cigar party this morning, with his doors flung open, and he and some other chaps saw Blythe come up the stairs and go into his own rooms with a beautiful, shapely, dark-haired woman with icy blue eyes, very pale, like a Scandinavian's, they said. All the chaps there watched them go in, most of them goggling in disbelief at the woman's unearthly splendour. This was at about ten o' clock. At quarter of an hour later, the smokers had all run out of matches, so Carruthers knocked on Blythe's door to ask if he could spare him a box of Lucifers.

'There was no answer.

'The door was ever so slightly ajar, so Carruthers pushed it open a little, popped his head around the edge, and called, "Are you there, Blythe?"

'It was then that he saw the body on the carpet, in front of the fireplace.

'It was utterly naked, spread-eagled in a supine position and bereft of all colour apart from the red imprint of a pair of sensuously full lips on the poor boy's breast.'

'Oh, I say. Good Lord.'

'Indeed. Well, Carruthers went in, growing in dismay; and when he caught sight of the tangled pile of red and pink blood vessels beside the corpse, he promptly vomited on the hearth rug.'

'And the beautiful lady?'

'Nowhere to be seen. She certainly hadn't gone down the stairs. The chaps across the landing had been watching out for her.'

'Perhaps she made her escape through the dormer? Along the parapet?'

'No, because Empson, the college handyman, was up there resealing the lead flashing between Blythe's room and the chapel roof, and he saw nobody. And on the other side of the sitting room, it's a thirty foot drop down onto flagstones. I doubt very much that the lady scaled down the wall.'

'How bizarre. May I see the body?' I asked.

Pedigree seemed astonished at my request, but took me to the morgue at Addenbrooke's Hospital on Trumpington Street.

'Ah,' said the attendant at the mortuary, recognising Edmund. 'You're the gentleman as what's Tutor of Case Number 3, the peculiar one as came in earlier today from the Constabulary.'

With a bow, the chap led us into a freezing cold room of white and green tiles, stone slabs and steel instruments.

Four bodies lay shrouded by long white sheets.

"Ere we are, then, gen'lemen,' said the attendant, cheerily, whipping the sheet off the corpse as if he were performing a magical trick at a circus.

I surveyed the corpse with some distaste.

There was a look of surprise on the young man's face, and the kiss mark on his chest. Otherwise, I could see only the pathologist's incisions. I began to feel a little sick when I noticed several buckets of blood under the table, and an enamel tray bearing the whole of the fellow's venous system.

'Professor Brown, our pathologist, says there ain't no scientific explanation,' whispered the attendant, as he pulled the sheet back across the table. 'None at all. Weird, eh?'

'So, you can see why I've called you in, Monty,' added Pedigree, grimly.

'Oh, come, come. I'm just a scribbler of tales, neither a clergyman nor a medical man. I've no idea what's happened here.'

***

Edmund Pedigree invited me back to his rooms at Adonai for a restorative sherry. He had only just uncorked the bottle – a rather agreeable Moscatel, I noticed – 'we need the sugar to help us deal with the shock of seeing young Blythe like that,' he sighed - when we heard a man screaming in Old Court, outside.

'What the deuce?' cried Pedigree.

He flung open a window on that side of the room.

The noise was coming from the doorway of the Junior Common Room. A porter, who had been delivering the afternoon mail to the undergraduates' pigeon holes, was bellowing there in evident distress, gulping for air between his hysterical exhalations.

'What on earth's the matter, Fuller,' shouted Pedigree.

'It's Mr Lawlor, sir,' gasped the wild-eyed porter, looking up. 'He's gone, sir.'

'Gone?'

'You know, he's … gone.'

Pedigree ran out and down the stairwell into Old Court. I followed, with considerably less speed, but quickly enough to see Edmund push the porter to one side and stride into the Common Room.

Instinctively, I knew that we should find a horrid thing.

I was correct.

The young man Lawlor lay quite naked on the bare beer-stained floorboards of the common room, supine and spread-eagled, with a tangle of white fibrous nervous tissue piled up beside him. I could make out the thick trunk of the spinal cord and what I assume were the major nerves of the four limbs. Most gruesome of all was the apparently deliberate placing of the fellow's eyeballs, both still attached to their respective optic nerves, on top of this mound of nervous tissue as if they were some sort of rococo decoration.

The whole business looked to me like the work of a maniac.

Pedigree broke our shocked silence.

'Good Lord, look,' he said, pointing.

On Lawlor's breast was the perfect muddy pawmark of a dog.

Fuller, the porter, tip-toed up to us and gazed wide-eyed again at the remains.

'I saw him go in with a golden retriever just a minute since,' he whispered. 'A beautiful dog it was, real friendly like, a-wagging of its tail as if its dinner depended on it, nuzzling up to Mr Lawlor's hand all loving.'

'But where is the dog now?' I asked.

'Damn me if I know,' said the porter.

'Fuller!' cried Pedigree.

'Well, I'm sorry, Dr P,' protested the porter, 'but I feel all unnerved by what I've seen.'

Pedigree stared at the fellow, incredulous.

'Well,' said I, looking around carefully, 'there's no sign of a dog here. And the back door is clearly bolted, top and bottom. The windows are fully closed too.'

'I never saw it come out,' asserted Fuller. 'God help us! There's a devil in the college!'

'Let's not leap to conclusions,' I murmured.

'This is bad news for the First VIII,' continued the porter, 'and them just getting ready for the Lent Bumps an' all. Why, Mr Blythe, who died this morning of a vicious murder by beings unknown, was bow of the First VIII, and now here's Mr Lawlor, number 2 of the same boat, with his nerves all filleted through his empty eye sockets.'

Pedigree swore under his breath.

'Fuller, will you shut up, and go and call the police?' he snapped.

'I'll need a pay rise to cover my doctor's fees if this business carries on,' muttered Fuller, as he made his way back to the porters' lodge and the telephone.

'So, did this vanishing retriever dog belong to Lawlor?' I asked Pedigree.

'No, I don't think so,' said my colleague. 'He can't have kept one here, in his rooms. College regulations forbid it. The servants would have been bound to notice.'

We were staring in bewilderment at the corpse when we heard a young voice cry, behind our backs, 'Great God in Heaven!'

We turned abruptly.

A short and slender young man was near to tears behind us.

'Ah, Chambers,' said Dr Pedigree. 'You shouldn't have seen this.'

The young man groaned and cried, 'First Blythe, and now Lawlor. Someone's wiping out the whole VIII, aren't they?'

'Come, come, that's over-dramatic,' counselled Pedigree. 'Monty, this is Nathanael Chambers, cox of our First VIII.'

But Chambers wouldn't be consoled.

'Don't you see?' he insisted. 'It's systematic.'

'How do you mean?' I asked.

'Blythe was bow, otherwise known as number one. Lawlor was number two. What's the betting that Charlie Prod is the next victim?'

'He occupies the third seat?' I asked.

'Exactly. My God, I'd better warn him.'

Chambers turned smartly on his heel and sprinted out of the room.

'But why,' I said, turning back to Pedigree, 'would anyone want to exterminate your First VIII?'

The scientist shrugged his shoulders.

'It doesn't make any sense,' he replied. 'We're dealing with either a madman, or ... '

He stopped, and stared at me.

'A demon,' I continued.

'Good Lord,' burst out Pedigree. 'This is the twentieth century! King Edward's on the throne, not King Solomon! We know all the laws of physics apart from a few little wrinkles like the ultraviolet catastrophe, which Planck of Berlin is well on the way to clearing up. And yet ... '

'Exactly,' I said. 'Nobody knows how these internal organs can possibly have been extracted from the dead men's bodies without causing gross damage to other tissues. Yet their bodies appear to be intact, even the systems that have been removed.'

'It's all been done so quickly too,' added Pedigree.

'You obviously doubt whether there can be a natural explanation, or you wouldn't have asked me to come here.'

Pedigree winced.

'How I yearn for the comforting feel of a slide-rule in my hand right now,' he muttered.

Young Chambers came skidding back into the room, pursued by a tall and brawny young man who, of course, could have been none other than the Charlie Prod already mentioned.

I could see the colour drain from Prod's ruddy complexion as he gazed at the components of his friend, John Lawlor.

'Damn it, Chambers, why did you bring me here?' he cursed, stepping backwards.

'Because you're next,' warned the young coxswain.

I tutted. 'Now, now, you're basing this theory on a coincidence, my boy,' I said.

'I think not, sir,' said Chambers. 'Most undergraduates live in college. Let's suppose that this is the work of some assassin picking off undergraduates at random. What's the probability of two victims chosen at random both being members of the First VIII? Considerably less than a half of one percent, I'd say.'

'Good Heavens,' I cried. 'You're not one of these new-fangled statisticians, are you?'

Chambers smiled weakly. He shook his head.

'But he's right,' insisted Pedigree. 'In fact, if one asks what the probability is of rower number 1 in particular being selected out of the two hundred or so men in college, and then number 2 also being selected, the probability of this happening purely at random becomes vanishingly small.'

'This is all Persian to me,' snapped Prod, 'but I know it's not safe here. I can feel the peril in my bones. I'm going down until the whole disgusting business is cleared up.'

'Where to?' asked Chambers.

Prod snorted, then laughed mirthlessly.

'I'm not going to tell you *that*,' he replied.

***

Saturday 14th February 1903

The police have made extensive enquiries about whether the two dead oarsmen had any mortal enemies, but they have turned up nothing of any significance.

His Majesty's Coroner opened an inquest yesterday but then adjourned it immediately in sheer puzzlement at the pathologist's report. He said that that there would be no point in swearing in a jury until the police investigation is complete.

I have gone back to my Directorial desk at the Fitzwilliam Museum, where I am attempting to purchase an original 1215 copy of Magna Carta, complete with King John's seal, from the estate of the late Sir Roger Devereux, 8th Baronet, of Crumpton Hall, Rutland, whose ancestors were by tradition usually the High Sheriff of that Soke. However, the executors are demanding the exorbitant sum of £20,000 sterling for it, which would be enough to keep His Majesty the King supplied with cigars for the rest of his life, and long may he reign over us. I really do not know how I will find so much money, and the dowager Lady Devereux has pointedly told me that an American motor car manufacturer and a Russian Grand Duke are also very keen to buy the Charter.

I am writing a letter to the cultural attaché at the British Embassy in Constantinople about the Hegesippus manuscript. He is a Kingsman, and I hope, therefore, to be able to get him to go to Rodosto for me and locate the document personally – if it exists.

That fraud, Adolf Nitschmann, of All Angels College, has taken himself off to Heidelberg, doubtless to comfort himself with Dunkelbier and Glückwürst, following the right royal savaging I gave him in *Patristics Quarterly* over his shoddy attempt to identify various Hebraisms behind the Greek of dear old Eusebius's discussion of Hegesippus in his *Church History*. I doubt very much if the obscure Greek word Oβλιας, Oblias, as used of the upright James the Just, originally meant 'tent pole' in Hebrew, as the idiot Nitschmann absurdly claims.

I must have a glass of sherry.

I had a disagreeable dream last night about a drowned woman. Whenever I stop writing to ponder the extraordinary events of the last few days, the image of her softened face floats to the top of my mind and bobs up and down there, green weeds deeply entangled and waving amid her unkempt grey hair. I feel that I know the face, but cannot place it. And I have seen no recent reports of any drowned lady in the newspapers, local or national.

I am glad to say - there have been no more deaths among the young men of Adonai.

No-one has heard from Charlie Prod.

***

Tuesday 17th February 1903

I had just finished breakfast this morning when Tomkins the porter came up to me.

'There's a telephone communication for you, sir,' he announced.

'Can I take it in the Parlour?' I asked.

'Yes, sir. I've made the instrument ready for you.'

I went through to the Parlour and picked up the device.

'Hullo,' I announced. 'Dr Montague Rhodes James speaking.'

A gruff sort of fellow with a strong North Country accent was on the line.

'This is Hubert Prod, woollen manufacturer, of Bradford, Yorkshire,' he announced. 'I won't beat about the bush, Dr James. I have a particular favour to ask of you; and I shall certainly be the best friend you've ever had in your whole life if you're kind enough to grant it, sir.'

'Oh, really? What is this favour?'

'I should like you to come an' stay at my house on Baildon Moor ... and save my son.'

The bold voice wavered over this last clause.

My stomach turned through several revolutions, for I realised at once that the rip in the fabric of Nature that we had seen at Adonai College was still not repaired. Trouble was afoot in the West Riding. Moreover, I seemed to be regarded by diverse folk - without good reason, in my view - as the one man who might have the gift of being able to mend it. But I am merely a collector, and inventor, of curious tales.

'My dear fellow,' I replied, eventually, 'I'm sorry, but I fear you need a clergyman; and I am not myself in holy orders, I am simply a scholar.'

'No, no, no - you have a unique knowledge of all that is weird. I know that. You cannot deny it, sir.'

'But I have work to do here, Mr Prod. I am the Director of the Fitzwilliam Museum, and I am in the midst of a most delicate negotiation about the purchase of a national treasure.'

'Eh? What's that, then?'

'I am not at liberty to disclose the details, but I will say, to give you a sense of the scale of the thing, that it will be one of the most expensive acquisitions the Museum ever makes.'

'Well, then, let me help your Museum, Dr James.'

'I beg your pardon?'

'If you'll help me, I'll help you. To the value o' twenty thousand pounds.'

'Goodness! That is a lifetime's salary!'

'All you have to do is come to my house on Baildon Moor and I'll give your Museum a draft for the first ten thousand pounds straight away. And if you sort out young Charlie, God help him, the second ten thousand 'll follow just as soon as I'm sure he's safe. Of course, I'll also defray all your personal expenses, and pay you an allowance of a guinea a day while you're away from home.'

'Oh, I say. That is most generous,' I sighed.

'Well?'

'Yes, I'll come.'

'Today?'

'Yes. I can leave in an hour.'

'Excellent. Come to Baildon station. Telegraph me at PRODWOOL BRADFORD with the time o' your arrival and I'll meet you there with my motor car. A Daimler. The best for you, Dr James.'

***

How tiresome is this journey? Even the fastest route requires changes at Ely, Peterborough, Leeds, Shipley, and Bradford Midland, before getting an evening train to Baildon. I am somewhere between Peterborough and Leeds now, and not very happy, for the light in the carriage is poor for reading, and the heating is only intermittently good. My eyes are sore and my hands are cold. I think I shall try to sleep. I am so glad that I am wearing my warmest greatcoat.

***

I woke just as we began to slow down for Leeds. While I had been sleeping, the heating had become oppressive, and at a whistle blast I emerged from an uneasy dream full of lumbering dark shapes that encircled and overarched and suffocated me. When the train stopped, I fled from the carriage to the lavatory on the station platform, and washed my weary face in a sink full of cold water. As I finished drying myself, I glanced down into the liquid and saw, to my consternation, the rippled image of the drowned woman staring up at me again with those vacant pale-blue eyes. I gasped in alarm and fled to the bustling crowd on the platform.

***

I want to turn back, but I sense there will be no end to this business if I do.

***

Hubert Prod was waiting for me with his pony and trap in the yard of Baildon station. I recognised him immediately, for he was an older, stouter and, I think, more genial version of his son Charlie.

'Aye, you're Dr James, beyond a shadow,' he nodded, beckoning me with his whip. 'Jump up.'

'Is it far to your place?' I asked, passing my bag up.

'Nought but a couple o' mile or so,' he said, 'and don't fret, the first dollop o' t' money's in your bank account already.'

'Oh, I'm not fretting, sir.'

'Well, you're a gentleman, but if you're in business, like me, you learn quick enough that the thing most folk are particular about is prompt payment. Now, hold tight. Off, Jenny!'

The trap lurched forward.

'You actually live on the moor?' I asked.

'Aye. In a grand 'ouse. In all t' senses o' t' word.'

I studied Prod's face in the light of the lamp fixed on a pole beside him. There was no guile in the man, in my view, just energy, directness, perseverance, ambition.

After a minute or two, the cottages and villas along the roadside, with their pleasantly lamp-lit yellow windows, petered out and gave way to the rock and grass and bracken of the local moorland. The vehicle slowed as the horse began to labour up a gradual but nevertheless demanding incline.

'Where does this road go to?' I asked.

'Bingley, ultimately. But we'll stop on t' top o' Baildon Moor.'

'Is that where your son is?'

'I'll be damned if I know where Charlie is, Dr James.'

'Oh, dear.'

'Look, I might as well tell you t' story 'ere and now as in t' comfort o' my own home, if only to save my wife Martha from another fit o' useless blubberin'.'

'I'm so sorry.'

'Well, it's like this. My son came home from Cambridge in t' small hours o' Friday the 13th, very agitated, very alarmed, always wi' his chin o'er his shoulder, sayin' "Summat diabolical's afoot, Dad," and how he needs to keep himsel' well hidden. Don't mistake me, Dr James, he was glad to be home, all right, but he was ever vigilant, quite restless, you know?

'He's been saddlin' up his horse, Bessie, and going riding over t' moor all hours o' day and night, riding furiously but randomly, from what I can make out. He spends all day out there, wi' just a bit o' meat and a sip or two to keep him alive, ranging all o'er t' place, from 'ere north to Ilkley, he says, and west to Haworth and even beyond into bloody Lancashire, if you can believe that; God knows where else!

'Anyhow, Saturday night, he comes back all pensive, like, and shuts himself up in his room with a bottle o' Scotch. In his liquor, he shouts something about "a prison, not a bloody cottage" and "Abaddon", whatever in God's name that is. Well, the lad's door's well and truly locked, but when he starts screamin' his head off like that, I don't hesitate, me, Dr James – I just smash my way in, and ask what the Devil he means by all this rubbish he's shouting?

'His reply is, "Get Dr James, Dad. Monty James of King's. He'll know what to do."

'And so, I have. Do my lad's words mean anything to you, sir?'

I shrugged my shoulders in the darkness.

'I can only conjecture, at this stage,' I said. 'Where is the boy now?'

'Out. Riding o'er t' moor, I'll be bound.'

'But he'll be home later?'

'Who knows, sir? Who knows?'

***

A grand fire blazed in the living room of Prod Hall.

'There's a buffet in the dining room, if you'd like to eat,' said my host, handing me a glass of brandy and water. 'You'll forgive me for not offering you a sit-down meal, but we're all a bit on edge. Can't eat much. Cook's done some hot bits and pieces for you though.'

'Is Mrs Prod at home?' I asked.

'As I said, she's unwell,' replied my host, curtly.

'Of course.'

I took a sip of my drink.

Glancing through the huge front windows, I could see snow starting to fall heavily.

'Oh,' I began to exclaim at the prettiness of the scene, but quickly suppressed my delight.

Prod senior, looking outside, understandably became agitated.

'Come back, lad,' he muttered, at the window. 'Oh, come back, damn you.'

I stared down at my brandy and water in embarrassment.

In the liquid, I saw the left eye of the drowned woman, staring back up at me coldly.

I dropped the glass.

'Oh, I'm so sorry,' I apologised.

'Don't fret,' said my host, picking up the empty glass and wiping the carpet clumsily with the toe of his right boot. 'We're all on edge.'

What on earth is the meaning of this recurring vision I have?

'So, can you make nothing of my son's words?' asked Prod, after a long silence. 'What is this Abaddon that he speaks of?'

'Oh, it's a demon, in biblical and apocryphal literature. Thought to be associated with sloth.'

'Sloth? Sloth? But my Charlie's a hard-working lad.'

I held up my hands.

'These things are unfathomable,' I said, hurriedly. 'I shouldn't worry about it.'

I had, of course, decided to spare Prod senior the alarming details of the demonology. It is true that in the *Lanterne of Light*, dated about 1410, and attributed to Wycliffe, Abaddon is named as the demon of sloth. However, he is also, in rendering the Hebrew scriptures into English, correctly named as 'Destruction', and in the Revelation of St John the Divine he is named in Greek as Apollyon, the Lord of the Bottomless Pit and tormentor of the damned. The apocryphal writings of the Coptic Church add that he will lead the Damned to the destroying fires of hell. The margin of the Latin Vulgate names him 'Exterminans', which speaks for itself.

But what has Prod done – and, presumably, Blythe and Lawlor before him, or with him – to deserve the attention of this inventively and delicately gutting demon? If there is a demon in the case, which I am reluctant to concede at this stage.

Prod senior stared at me accusingly, as if he knew me to be holding back information. I was at a loss as to how to defuse the growing tension between us, and began to perspire uncomfortably, when a low moan and then a great wail from Mrs Prod somewhere above our heads broke the unbearable silence.

'I must bid you good night,' said my host, suddenly.

He turned on his heel and left, taking both oil lamps with him.

By the light of the coal fire, I found some candles and lit one. I made my way across the hall and into the dining room, where I tucked into a plate of cooked sausages.

The shadows from my candle often seemed to dance around me grotesquely, but, if truth be told, the near-darkness delighted me, for it meant that I was not able to see that ghastly dead woman's face in any reflective surface that my eye happened to chance upon.

Crossing back to the lounge, the candle flared up so suddenly and so brilliantly that I was afraid someone had concealed a bundle of Lucifers in the wax. When the candle guttered out, the darkness was even more intense.

I had to grope my way to bed, praying that I had remembered the way.

***

Wednesday 18th February 1903

I did not sleep well. I write this by the window in the grey light.

***

Morning, thank God.

We go in the pony and trap to explore the roads & paths over the moor.

I have still not met Mrs Prod.

Utterly white out here. Prod has a telescope with which he surveys the scene.

'Got him! There he is, the young devil, galloping on his horse. Do you see him, Dr James? Black against the snow. Unmissable.'

I can see a speck in the distance, moving rapidly over the freezing landscape.

'If we go up Wyke Track, we can cut him off,' says Prod.

We find a tiny stone cottage a little to the side of the Track, nestling in a slight concavity of the moor. Smoke curls up into the frosty air from the chimney.

'I thought this place was derelict,' says Prod.

Yet the door is wide open, giving us a glimpse of a blazing fire within.

'Hang on a minute,' says my host.

He jumps down from the trap & strides over to the door.

'The lad's been here,' he announces. 'Those are his books on t' table. Bloody Edgar Allan Poe. That's what's been feedin' 'is morbid imagination, I'll be bound.'

Prod searches the snow around for human tracks & begins to follow some.

I walk into the modest parlour & look around. Despite the log fire, the room is very cold & thick ice clings to the windows inside. I gasp as I glance at the panes, for on each of them there seems to be a sketch in frozen water of the drowned woman who haunts my glances. How in Heaven's name can that be?

The cottage is a woman's. No doubt about that. The clothes. The furnishings. A photograph stands on a sideboard. I raise it to my eyes & inspect it. It consists of two people, a man & a woman, both of roughly the same age, side by side in front of a tall column. With a jolt, I realise that I know one of them! By Jupiter, it is Adolf Nitschmann of All Angels College, who has just gone scurrying back to Germany with his tail between his legs because of my exposé of his nonsense over the word $O\beta\lambda\iota\alpha\varsigma$. Tent-pole indeed! But who is the woman?

I study her face closely. My heart suddenly freezes.

Surely this is the woman whose lifeless face has been disturbing me? And, seeing her face here with Adolf Nitschmann, I can only think – from the likeness – that she must be his sister?

In the bedroom, there are two more photographs, one of the fraudster Nitschmann and the other of the dead woman. Yes, I'm sure of this now. Brother and sister. They're so very alike, now that I can rotate the portraits through various angles and compare them carefully.

I go back to the parlour. There is a small bookcase. I see the three Brontë sisters, Mrs Gaskell's book on Charlotte, Shelley the wife, Mrs Radcliffe, Clara Reeve, Mrs Riddell.

Gothic women!

Here is a copy of the issue of *Patristics Quarterly* that contains Nitschmann's paper on the meaning of the word Oblias. And a reprint of it in the *Proceedings of the Royal Swedish Fraternity for Sacred Scripture*, of which I've never heard before. What an absurd argument the fellow uses.

Οβλιας is imperfectly transliterated from the Hebrew, he says, so we don't know what the original was. But it evidently designates James the Just as a source of strength, a pillar, or wall, or bulwark, or fortress as Eusebius and Epiphanius suggest. But the *Οβ, Ob,* is quite possibly a poor transliteration of the Hebrew אב, in English *Ab,* meaning father or head of the house, drawing on the ancient (that is, archaic) Hebrew meanings of 'ox' for א and 'tent' for ב, which taken together signify the strength of the tent, literally, the tent-pole, which also symbolises the strength of the head of the house - in this case, of the head of the Jerusalem Church, namely, James the brother of the Lord. All quite absurdly speculative, as I pointed out in my rejoinder in the subsequent issue. Tish! Look at how violently Nitschmann has crossed out and defaced my critique. His pen has nearly cut through the paper, so heavy was his wrathful hand.

What's this?

Rummaging further, I find a complete manuscript of Hegesippus' *Five Commentaries on the Acts of the Church* in Nitschmann's own hand on modern paper, with a pencil note on it saying, simply, 'Mar Gabriel Monastery, Tur Abdin, Ottoman Empire.' But surely this is just an invention of Nitschmann's? However, I must note that there is also a rather creased photograph here of the first page of a Greek text of the same document, which, insofar as one can tell from a reproduction of such poor quality, looks like a Byzantine uncial. But this photograph has nothing to say on the Oblias question.

Here is a manuscript of a novel, in a similar hand to the purported Hegesippus, which appears to be some kind of Brontë-like novel about a clergyman ruining himself with a serving girl at a moorland inn. Tosh!

A young voice from the threshold.

'I keep seeing the face of a woman who drowned in the Cam.'

It is Prod junior. He walks into the room and opens a cupboard. He tears a chunk of bread from a stale looking loaf and thrusts it into his mouth.

'You see it looking back at you from water?'

'Yes,' he says. 'Is that common?'

Strange question.

'I've no idea. But I've seen it too.'

'You? But you weren't there.'

'Where?'

'At the river, when we saw her.'

'You'll have to explain, young man.'

'The First VIII. We'd been out carousing at *The Sleeping Duck* near the boat club. We were staggering back along the river bank on Jesus Green when we saw a woman jump off the foot bridge into the water. Or rather, Chambers did. The rest of us were too busy laughing at a dirty joke Blythe had just told us. We heard the splash of course, but just thought it was someone chucking rocks into the water. But Chambers insisted that he'd seen a middle-aged woman with grey hair jump in. We were advising him not to make such an ass of himself when we heard a woman cry, "No!", from the water.

'Well, we all ran to the edge and stared into the rippling darkness. "Please!" came a second cry. We heard some splashing, like limbs flailing. Lawlor took off his shoes and trousers, sat on the bank and thrust his legs into the water. "Too bloody cold," was his verdict. He pulled his legs out again and just said, "Hmm."

'"Please," came the woman's voice from the river. We all stared but could see no-one. Then Blythe said, "Silly bugger, can't even make her mind up about killing herself."

'At that, we all fell about laughing on the grass, and rolled around with shrieks of merriment while the cries grew fainter and fewer and finally stopped altogether.'

Chilling.

Charlie Prod goes into the bedroom & returns with the photograph of the woman.

'This is who I see,' he says, waving the picture at me.

I nodded.

'As do I.'

Now Prod senior snorts from the doorway.

'A fine help you are,' he cries at me. 'You're as addled as the lad is. And as for you, Charlie, do you mean to tell me that by some strange miracle you happen to have found here, on Baildon Moor, a cottage belonging to a woman who drowned herself in a river, some two hundred miles away, and were just able to waltz in, without so much as a by-your-leave, and make yourself at home?'

A long pause before the boy says, 'I didn't find the cottage, father. It found me.'

A harsh laugh. 'A remarkably intelligent pile of stones and mortar, then, my lad.'

'It was my horse, sir. I couldn't get it to go anywhere but here initially.'

'Who on earth does this place belong to?' demands Prod senior, gazing around.

'A scholar of Gothic literature, I should think,' says the boy. 'One with a particular interest in the Brontë sisters.'

I remember now. Adolf Nitschmann is a Brontë enthusiast too. He's written several monographs on the dialectic of Christianity and paganism in their works. I've read his papers. Highly speculative. Far too much reliance on occasional words and phrases.

Where is Nitschmann?

Perhaps I should cable him care of Heidelberg University?

Warn him that his sister is missing?

***

The beastly cottage door slammed on my right hand. I cannot write with it. I must make do as best I can with my left hand. If some malicious spirit thinks that it will stop my scholarly efforts by such a *poltergeistlich* trick, then it is much mistaken.

The wind caught the door as I was crossing the threshold to look at young Prod's horse. My accident seemed to spook the boy and he darted out himself and sprang to the stirrup.

But how did the wind blow from the inside of the cottage to do that? Perhaps it was a trick of air pressure across the doorway? I know so little of natural science.

The woollen manufacturer and I scrambled up a hillock and watched the boy gallop away across the snows of the moor. I do not care to record the Yorkshireman's oaths and curses.

'Look,' he cried, pointing, 'what's that?'

I could see nothing in the direction indicated but a gently sloping expanse of snow and ice rising to meet dark grey cloud. The air around us seemed ripe for bursting.

'What do you mean?'

'It's a horse and rider, I'm sure of it, following Charlie. Don't you see it?'

'No.'

'Well, a white horse against snow isn't the easiest thing to see, I grant you.'

'A white horse?'

'Yes.'

I looked again, particularly hard this time, and managed to see the beast. Of course, I thought immediately of the Book of Revelation chapter 6 verse 8, and took in my breath sharply.

'What's the matter?' asked Prod senior.

I could not stop myself from quoting the text.

'And I looked, and behold a pale horse: and his name that sat on him was Death, and Hell followed with him.'

Prod turned fearful eyes upon me.

'What the devil do you mean?' he cried.

I did not answer but turned my own gaze towards the figure of Prod junior.

'Tell me,' insisted Prod.

'Oh, it may not signify. Your words just stirred my memory, that's all.'

'May not?'

The boy rode his black horse fiercely over the moor, but I noticed that the white horse and its blanched rider sought not so much to catch up with young Prod, as to nudge him in a certain direction. And that direction, no matter where on the snow-clad moor the two horses were, was always pointing back to Nitschmann's sister's cottage.

I pointed this observation out to Prod senior.

'Eh?' was his response. 'How do you make that out?'

But as the quarter-hours slid slowly by, it became evident that I was right, for young Prod was drawing ever closer to the cottage.

The white horse, as it neared us, looked utterly beautiful – graceful, elegant, dazzling – but from its mouth there erupted a plume of breath that seemed to indicate such a vacancy of space, such a void of light, as seemed to threaten the very fabric of reality around it. I could only watch in shivering horror as this exhalation of darkness from an animal of gleaming ice grew closer and closer to young Charlie Prod. And yet, the goal of the glinting rider seemed still not to be to overtake his young prey, but to steer him towards the cottage.

As the boy and his pursuer came close, I could feel my entrails twisting with anxiety.

The father, beside me, uttered such a cry as I hope never to hear again.

Charlie Prod jumped down from his horse. The beast bolted at once.

Now came the pale horse. Yes, it and its rider seemed as if made of ice. Transparent, perhaps, but so distorting as to twist space and delete all the information that light normally carries.

An intense cold surrounded us.

The three of us – Prod senior and junior and I – retreated into the cottage, and clustered in fear in front of the waning fire. Through the open doorway, we could see the pale horse shrinking away, as it seemed to me, until only an icy simulacrum of Adolf Nitschmann stood on the snow before the threshold.

Nitschmann, if that is who, or what, this figure was, stepped inside. In the flickering of the dying fire, it seemed to become nothing other than a cold black void in space, stretching out its arms, one to me, the other to young Prod.

'No!' cried Prod senior, and he threw himself on the blackness.

There was a flash of light and a hiss and an echoing sigh.

When I opened my eyes again, Prod senior had disappeared completely.

'Father!' cries the boy. 'Father!'

There is a frost burn on my arm, but the cottage feels warmer.

Charlie Prod runs outside, still calling for his father. All the while, as he calls, he is rubbing his chest. Finally, despairing, he tears open his shirt front and looks down at the locus of his irritation. The faint print of a horse shoe is forming there.

***

Friday 6th March 1903

I have written to Heidelberg but the only reply I have had is from the Herr Professor Doktor Ulrich von Spangenberg-Rixdorf, Dean of the Faculty of Theology, to say that Nitschmann has not been seen there for several years.

Nitschmann! I thought I caught sight of the blighter the other day in the University Library. I noticed a sort of more solid bit of shadow, near a cupboard in a corridor, that was oriented towards me in an accusing kind of way. I flung my pipe at the shadow and it vanished, though that might simply have been due to my own movement and the consequent change in the light from the window. I will dismiss the matter from my mind.

***

Tuesday 10th March 1903

Very bravely, young Prod has returned to Cambridge. He stayed in Yorkshire while the West Riding Constabulary carried out their searches for his father's body. But the Police have finally given up, and Prod senior has been declared missing, presumed dead.

The inquest into the deaths of Blythe and Lawlor re-opened yesterday. I have never seen a panel of jurymen so excited.

I invited Charlie Prod to tea today, and as we were eating our cucumber sandwiches there was a knock on my door.

I rose to open it.

From where he was sitting, Charlie could see through the open door to the staircase too. He uttered an astonished cry before my own brain could interpret what I saw.

'Nitschmann!' I yelled.

The German scholar stood there, as solid as the Tower of London, staring at me silently; and then he slowly raised his right arm and pointed his absurdly long index finger at me in the most accusing manner before gradually fading from view.

To encourage him not to return, I threw a full box of matches at him from my jacket pocket.

'My God,' cried the boy, behind me. 'That was the drowned woman.'

'What? You're mistaken, young Charlie. That was Adolf Nitschmann.'

'No, that was his sister, surely?'

We argued about the matter for ten minutes. Inconclusively.

Thursday 12th March 1903

I'm still undecided about who it was that knocked at my door.

Is the unquiet soul of Adolf Nitschmann, or of his sister, or of whoever else he or she happens to think he or she is, still wandering? I believe that it does, on occasion, if only to gape at me ineffectually and evanescently. One catches a glancing view of its miserable face from the corner of one's eye, when shaving or blowing one's nose or lighting a pipe.

I have said prayers for the soul's rest. I have asked others, holier men than I, to pile their worthier prayers on top of mine. Yet the soul still wanders, disconsolately. I have found a remedy of sorts, albeit a palliative rather than a cure, against its unwelcome incursions, namely, that a cup of tea, of highly scented China tea for preference, without milk and still scalding hot, when flung in the face of the apparition, will make it vanish instantly. Nothing else works! Neither Shakespeare nor Milton, neither pipe nor pouch, neither keys nor coins; not even a book-mark print of Holman Hunt's painting, *Lux Mundi,* that some dreadful woman gave me.

I'm sure there must be a law behind these things, but I'm damned if I know what it is.

Friday 29th May 1903

Is it a surprise? The Prod family have not remitted to me the promised balance of £10,000 and the Fitzwilliam Museum has therefore been compelled, regretfully, to let the Magna Carta be purchased by a motor car manufacturer in the United States.

Extensive enquiries have revealed no further trace of Adolf Nitschmann.

No body of a drowned woman with grey hair has been found in the River Cam, or the Great Ouse into which it feeds, or the North Sea.

Neither has the body of a drowned man, for that matter.

And young Charlie Prod and the other surviving hearties of the Adonai First VIII are still alive and rowing.

For now.

THE ORGAN OF CORPUSTY

Friday 20th September 1929

How lucky a fellow is when he is paid guineas to do things that give him the utmost pleasure. Here I am in Sall, or Salle, in Norfolk, a place I first visited in 1884 and to which I always return with delight. Today I am here to observe the glass, the carving and the painting in the parish church afresh for my new book, *Suffolk and Norfolk: A Perambulation of the Two Counties with Notices of their History and their Ancient Buildings*, which is to be published by J M Dent & Sons Ltd. The chancel roof is still a most beautiful specimen, with its exquisitely carved bosses; and though the tracery lights of the great east window seem to have been moved about somewhat, I can still detect the Nine Orders of Angels; notably the two *Principatus* and two *Dominations* with devils at their feet, and the two *Potestates* with subjugated red dragons. The east window of the south transept has the Annunciation in two lights, with the three local worthies who paid for it praying *Nos cum prole pia Benedicta virgo Maria*, May the Virgin Mary bless us with her holy child.

***

Saturday 21st September 1929

Gazing up at the chancel roof bosses in Sall seems to have made me rather giddy. I have had palpitations of the heart that, at their worst, were really quite alarming. My driver – kindly provided by Dent & Sons - feared that I was about to have a 'bloody coronary' and urged me to go to Norwich at once for treatment at the Norfolk & Norwich Hospital.

However, I had a much better idea. Not far from Sall, only four miles or so, is the village of Corpusty, where a young friend of mine from Cambridge, Cedric Fox-Bright, is the vicar. The living of Corpusty is in the gift of the Provost and Fellows of King's College, and when I was Provost I made sure that Fox-Bright - who had been invalided out of the Army Chaplaincy with a Military Cross after rescuing five badly wounded men from No Man's Land under heavy machine-gun fire - was presented to it. Quite apart from his bravery, Cedric is a first- rate patristics scholar, whom, I am proud to say, I taught myself. He has a profound knowledge of the works of the Pseudo-Dionysius and, in particular, a deep and, I should say, quite personal affinity with the great theologian's treatise *On Mystical Theology*.

Anyway, I had Jenkins, my driver, take me to the Corpusty vicarage, which stands opposite the water mill on the west bank of the River Bure, and deliver me to dear Fox-Bright, baggage and all. Of course, Cedric was delighted to see me; and his wife, whom I had met only once before, at their wedding, insisted that I should stay until I felt totally well. That, I fear, might prove to take rather a long time, but I gratefully accepted the offer of a south-facing room, and installed myself for a few days. Mrs Fox-Bright is not at all keen on tobacco, so I shall take a holiday from my pipe and ask the Almighty for clean lungs and a steady heart. Jenkins, refreshed with the gift of a gleaming sovereign, has gleefully taken himself off to the fleshpots of Norwich. I am looking forward to some charming conversation with my old protégé.

***

Sunday 22nd September 1929

Here I am at St Peter's, Corpusty. This church, with its sturdy tower, stands quite alone at the top of a rather tiresome hill, like some sentinel keeping watch over the Bure valley to prevent marauders from the sea-coast beyond Holt from reaching the Norwich road.

Why is the church so isolated, I wonder? The usual explanation for this kind of thing is that the Black Death destroyed the medieval village. But the solitary prominence of the church here on its hill is really rather eerie.

The church as a whole is pleasant but not very distinguished. It is mainly Perpendicular, though I think there are fragmentary remains of a Norman building in the walls here and there. The windows of nave and chancel date from the 14th century, the font and rood screen from the 15th. There is no pulpit, just a lectern; and there are no pews, just a few chairs and benches in nave and chancel alike.

Matins, read by Fox-Bright. It is a refreshingly simple service. The congregation is not large, as most people in the village find it more convenient to go to Saxthorpe Church, St Andrew's, which is just across the River Bure from the centre of Corpusty village. The congregation here, therefore, at the top of this remote-feeling eminence, consists of just a few conservative-minded farmers and their tenant labourers, who work the broad fields around St Peter's.

Divine service is read, not sung. This is despite the church having a fine organ, built in 1748 by Johann Schnetzler, the famous Swiss instrument maker. Peterhouse, Cambridge, has another one of his. The Corpusty organ, however, in a ruinous state. It was evidently once marvellous. Thirty pedals, and fifty-eight keys each on the great and swell organs, with many stops and couplers, eight-foot diapasons, a sixteen-foot bourdon and even a thirty-two-foot harmonic bass. Or so Cedric told me, after the service.

But the organ's now full of rust and rot, the cabinet cracked and breaking. Cedric's keen to get the blessèd wreck thundering again, but the churchwardens won't hear of it. They absolutely refuse to let him touch it! And only they have the keys to the organ loft.

The console is in a little gallery about ten feet above the ground at the back of the nave. The longer pipes are housed in the bottom of the church tower, which is also where the pump handle stands for the bellows-boy whose job it once was to fill the wind box.

I tried lifting this handle myself, but it seems to be disconnected from the bellows; or it might be that the bellows have so disintegrated that no resistance is offered to pumping?

'Be careful,' warned Cedric.

'Why?'

'The churchwardens – they'll cut your arm off, if they see you doing that!'

'What on earth are you talking about?'

'They're adamantly against the organ being played, Monty. Adamantly.'

'But why?'

'Because of a strange covenant made by their predecessors. They claim that if this covenant is ever broken, it will bring utter disaster to them personally and to the church, because of a threat made by the man who commissioned the organ in the first place.'

'And who was he?'

'Sir Roger Kettle, the lord of the manor around here in 1748. He had the instrument built as a sort of peace offering to his wife after the Battle of Culloden. Sir Roger, you see, was an ardent Hanoverian, loyal to King George II, whereas his wife, Lady Henrietta, née Murray, was a Scottish Episcopalian whose family were loyal to the Stuart Pretender. Indeed, two of her uncles were killed fighting for Bonnie Prince Charlie in 1746.

'The wife could scarcely forgive her husband for his support of the harsh policies of the Butcher Cumberland, who destroyed many a Highland family's noblest sons during and after the Jacobite Rising. But with her High Church sympathies, she loved anthems and the singing of versicles and responses, canticles, and psalms - and a rousing voluntary at the end of worship; and so, the husband commissioned Schnetzler to come and build a fine organ in this remote part of Norfolk.

'Thus, for a couple of years, marital harmony was restored, and the Lady Henrietta prayed for the souls of her lost uncles at the altar rail of Corpusty church, while Thomas Garland, the organist of Norwich Cathedral, or his assistant, Hezekiah Potter, played Bach fugues on the magnificent new organ. The Lady Henrietta loved these fugues, because, with their several intertwining voices, they seemed to her to symbolise the glorious inner life of the Most Holy Trinity. But this was not to last.

'In 1751, the Lady Henrietta, while walking to her carriage to return home after divine service, stumbled and in trying to steady herself cut her hand on a rusty nail that was protruding from the gatepost of the churchyard. She made light of this, but an infection set in, and she became feverish within a couple of days. The whole arm became inflamed, diabolical red streaks making their way to her breast; the wound itself emitted a foul odour, which no poultice could remove. The following Sunday, she died in her bed, groaning and ranting before being wrenched away to Purgatory in a dreadful final convulsion.

'Sir Roger was crushed by his loss. He mourned his wife not only for her great beauty, but also for the dignity, cheerfulness and good sense she had habitually shown. He had a vault dug for her remains just in front of the altar here in Corpusty church, beneath the spot where she had loved to kneel in prayer and commend the souls of her gallant uncles to the care of their Saviour.

'Into this crypt, after a tender funeral service in which the Cathedral organist played the magnificent dead march from Handel's *Saul* and Purcell's *Music for the Funeral of Queen Mary*, the latter sung by choristers brought in especially from Norwich, the Lady Henrietta's sturdy coffin was solemnly lowered. Great stones were then laid upon the vaulting of the tomb, sealing the dead woman away from the living.

'The next day, Sir Roger called the two churchwardens to his home at Corpusty Manor. He treated them to a sumptuous meal and as much ale as they felt that in all decency they could drink in the sad circumstances; and when the three of them sat together smoking their pipes by the blazing fire afterwards, he asked them to look over a solemn Deed & Covenant that he had already had his attorney in Norwich draw up.

'"What be this?" asked Jacob Wool, the vicar's warden.

'"An agreement," said the squire, "that the Schnetzler organ should never be played again until either we or our descendants hear the sound of the Last Trump."

'"But why?" protested Isaac Ember, the laymen's warden. "We should glorify God with that great organ, Sir Roger, for as long as we can, that's what I'm believing."

'"Aye," agreed Wool. "And what do the vicar to say to this?"

'"The vicar," replied Sir Roger, shortly, "agrees with whatever I propose. And I tell you, gentlemen, that I'm determined to have my way. The glory has passed away from the earth, and there must be no music now in Corpusty church, only sad solemn silence. And yet, I recognise that you and the other good folk of the parish deserve some compensation for the loss of the beauty of the sung liturgy in our dear church. For that reason, I propose to set up an Endowment that will benefit the poor and needy folk of this parish, to be governed and administered in perpetuity by the two churchwardens now in office and their lawful successors, in the name of the Lady Henrietta. And as governors of the Trust, you, Isaac Ember, and you, Jacob Wool, will be paid an honorarium each, and all reasonable expenses, from the annual interest on the fund, to a value that you as Christian gentlemen shall determine just and appropriate."

'Well, the two wardens acceded to this plan instantly. The deed was signed, and Sir Roger had the bellows disabled and the stairs up to the organ gallery blocked by this simulacrum of the Gates of Death.

'To this day, Monty, no-one has touched the organ whether to play or to maintain it, and as you have seen, it is but a ruin of its former self.'

'But you mentioned a threat?'

'Ah, yes. Sir Roger made no explicit provision in law for what should happen by way of penalty if the terms of the Covenant were breached. Jacob Wool later told his son that he had put this very question to the squire.

'"I have every faith in the good sense of the wardens," was his only answer.

'But on the morning of the day on which Sir Roger himself died, he summoned the two churchwardens to his sick bed.

'"I have seen the Lady Henrietta," he whispered, "standing by yonder wardrobe, a welcoming smile on her precious lips. My time is nigh, gentlemen."

'The wardens deprecated this statement.

'"No, no," cried Isaac Ember. "You'll get better, sir. It's only the north wind that's making you feel low of spirit."

'"I hear the wings of the angel," gasped the squire. "Let me warn you, gentlemen. If, for whatever reason, you or your successors break the terms of our Solemn Covenant, there will be a reckoning from beyond the grave. Beyond the grave! Do you hear me?"

'The two churchwardens were frightened by the sudden fire in Sir Roger's eyes, and nodded keenly, stepping away from him.

'The squire stared at them intently, then relaxed, sighed, and passed.

'And to this day, Monty, the churchwardens have forbidden anyone to touch the organ, whether to play it or even just to care for it. And do you know what?'

'What?'

'The names of the two churchwardens even today are - Wool and Ember.'

Cedric threw back his head and laughed at this little local absurdity.

Rather foolishly, I thought.

**

The thing about Cedric Fox-Bright is that he is one of these High & Modern types, who believe in both ritual and relevance, in the beauty of holiness and the ugliness of doctrine.

'We must communicate the Faith through art, Monty,' he told me, over a sweet sherry.

'I can see where you're heading with this,' I remarked, lighting my pipe.

Cedric spluttered in my clouds of delight.

'Is that thing good for you?' he queried.

'Oh, a chap can't live without a little pleasure,' I murmured.

'Anyway, where is it you think I'm heading?'

'You mean to restore the organ. It's as plain as the moustache on your face.'

'Absolutely, Monty! It's criminal to let a Schnetzler organ crumble away to dust.'

'So, you're not worried about a reckoning from beyond the grave?'

'Oh, I don't think anyone can know for sure about the Hereafter, so I don't really care, to be frank; and I'm certainly not worried about penalties on this side of the grave. The authorities at King's, who, as you know, hold the advowson for the living of Corpusty, say that I should do whatever I think is best for the parish. Then there's the Bishop. He has referred me to the Diocesan Solicitor, who says that the Deed of Covenant makes no provision for any penalties, other than that any man who abrogates it must look to the welfare of his own soul.'

'In other words, you think it's a moral rather than a legal matter?'

'Yes, I think so. And I mean to repair the organ out of my own pocket, of course. I've had plenty of money since my father died.'

'But that's irrelevant,' I pointed out. 'The significant thing is that you're going against the express wishes of the man who installed the organ, Sir Roger Kettle. He did not and does not want music at Divine Service. That is the end of the matter, surely?'

'Oh, come, come,' riposted Cedric. 'As our Lord said, "The Sabbath is made for man, and not man for the Sabbath." We should be free to order our worship as we please, and not be bound for all time by some obsolete covenant! I mean, dash it all, Monty, it isn't as if the Lady Henrietta's name is being forgotten, is it? Her charity will still help the poor. And I shall be able to beautify our services with her Schnetzler organ, which will win new souls for Christ through the divine music of His sacred drama!'

I removed the pipe from my mouth, and pointed the stem at Cedric.

'I should be very careful if I were you,' I advised.

'Oh, I think I know how to put the soul of Sir Roger to rest,' he smiled.

The cheery disposition and instinctive bravery that earned Fox-Bright the Military Cross in the trenches will not serve him so well in a tussle with the supernatural.

***

Tuesday 15th October 1929

How pleasant it is to be back in the Provost's lodgings at Eton. I sit by the fire with a small dry sherry and divert myself by reading St Jerome's irate abuse of rich widows with red lips and plump sleek skins, whose houses are full of flatterers and whom the clergy kiss on the forehead before holding out a hand for the fee they charge for their pastoral visit.

Jerome is perhaps not a model of Christian charity, but he is a superb Latin stylist – and one cannot fault his conviction.

I have received a letter from Cedric Fox-Bright, which I append.

My dear Monty,

I am making progress with my plans, despite opposition.
First of all, the churchwardens tried to confuse me.
'Why does this Covenant exist?' I asked them.
They didn't really know why.

'It's because the organ was badly built and unpleasing to the ear,' said Wool. 'It used to irritate Lady Henrietta.'

'I always thought it was because Sir Roger believed nobody could ever play it better than she did,' said Ember. 'He wanted money to go on preserving the church as a whole as her Ladyship's mausoleum, rather than on preserving just the organ, you see?'

'Yes, that's right, that is, about the church as a whole,' chimed Wool.

Then, when this didn't convince me, they tried to play on my sense of charity, and said that I'd be the death of many a poor parishioner who relied on the Kettle Trust for winter fuel. But they relented when I said that payments from the Trust would continue as before, and that if there is to be any opprobrium as a result of this change, then I alone should incur it.

At this, they consented to my proposal, though rather ungraciously.

And they refused to help in any way with the restoration of the instrument.

My first act was to try and mend the bellows myself. While I was doing this, I was troubled by a large raven that kept tapping the glass in the west window of the tower, and staring at me with what I can only describe as a disgusted look on its little face. Every time I put my hand to any part of the organ, the bird pecked even more vigorously at the window until the rat-a-tat-tat on the glass sounded like nothing more than a Gerry machine gun sweeping deadly fire back and forth across Corpusty churchyard.

Why the bird was so interested in my business, I do not pretend to know.

The main problem with the bellows was that the leather had become detached from the wood in various places. The leakage was very evident from just lifting the handle a couple of times. I ran my right index finger along the joins to get a better sense of the scale of the damage, and suddenly tore the pad of my finger on something sharp – you should have heard me, Monty! Such an oath! And in my own church too! I was dripping blood, and had to tie a handkerchief around the shredded skin.

I abandoned the bellows and went to the steps that led up to the gallery. A heavy wooden gate blocked the entrance to the narrow staircase, and was secured with an ancient padlock for which I had not been able to find the key. I shook the gate, thinking that I could probably break either the lock or the hinges. The thing looked pretty worm-eaten, after all. But a most peculiar thing happened. I was tugging on the gate and shaking it when someone or something kicked my feet from beneath me, from behind. I fell flat on my back and, though winded for a moment, leapt up sharply so that I could turn and see who it was that had assaulted me.

You've guessed, no doubt! No-one was there. Quite! The church was empty, apart from myself. I examined the stones of the floor carefully, but I could detect no reason why my feet should have suddenly lost their purchase on the ground! I was not to be deterred by this strange event, so I vaulted over the old gate and ran up the stairs to the organ loft two steps at a time. But just as I reached the gallery, and could see the yellowing keys of the two manuals before me, a six-foot organ pipe above my head gave a tired sigh and toppled forwards, whacking me on my right shoulder like some Argyll & Southerland Highlander with a knobkierie!

No chance of playing the treble clef properly now, old man! But look, there's something dashed odd about all this, and I've invited a big chief from the Society for Psychophysical Research in London to come down here and check the place out. It has bad vibrations, Monty, I can tell you, and I'm sure the SPR boffins will have some device or other for damping them down! Well, I certainly hope so! It *would be such good fun if you could be here too. Their man, a very eminent physicist from Scotland, I believe, will be here on 21st of this month if you'd care to join us?*

Do come! And of course, let me know if you're coming, so we can prepare.

***

Monday 21st October 1929

Of course, I was not able to keep away from Corpusty.

The great physicist from the Society for Psychophysical Research was none other than its President, Lord Crankshaft, an expert on thermodynamics (as he told me himself). A huge, tall, commanding fellow with a beard like the prophet Isaiah and a booming preacher's voice to match, he believes, with the philosopher Spinoza, that all mental events have a physical counterpart, and all physical events a mental one; and as his own peculiar contribution to this doctrine, he argues that subtle changes in the random distribution of heat energy in the atmosphere connect the brain and the world in hidden – one might say, occult - ways.

Crankshaft says that these 'little marshallings' of random heat in the air and in the objects around us are quite additional, of course, to the normal physical action of the human body through its muscles. They are not, he adds, generally subject to conscious control. However, I cannot take them seriously as an explanation of the occult. Yes, one might, in principle, be able to slice up a sirloin steak with a sufficiently concentrated jet of steam conjured up somehow by the power of the mind. But is that of any practical relevance to real life? How often can it be done? Ye gods, I can scarcely influence my own hands these days, let alone remote objects!

Surely the much deeper issue in these matters is the power of Malevolence to subvert all order in the universe, mental and physical?

***

Crankshaft surveyed the interior of Corpusty church like a magnificent stag on a crag.

'Splendid!' he cried, tapping the flagstones with his steel-tipped cane. 'This is a most interesting problem. It is clear to me that the source of the opposition to your plan of using the organ again after all these years is your own unconscious mind, Mr Fox-Bright. Are you familiar with the work of Professor Freud of Vienna and his disciples, sir?'

'Never heard of him,' said Cedric (which I do not for a moment believe).

'Well, I'd say that you're a man in two minds about your own project, sir; and there is no greater expert in the world about the many compartments of a human mind - and their mutual antagonisms - than the great psychologist Sigmund Freud.

'But how does the unconscious mind exert its hidden effects, gentlemen? That is where I as a physicist come in. Yes, as a physicist!

'Your own body, Mr Fox-Bright, is the culprit. It is taking heat from the atmosphere of the church, as well as from the food in your own stomach, and is projecting this heat towards the objects about which you feel ambivalent - namely, the components of the church organ, that *consciously* you wish to restore but *unconsciously* you would prefer to see mouldering away in a silence like that of the tomb. That's why the organ pipe toppled onto your shoulder, sir.'

'But now, look here,' protested Cedric, 'why on earth should my unconscious mind want to let the organ rot? That's absurd!'

'I suspect there are psychosexual forces at play here that are very powerful, my dear sir, but which it would be most indelicate of me to explore further with you, given your cloth.'

'What utter nonsense!' cried Cedric. 'I know my own mind fully!'

I coughed politely, hoping to discharge the tension before it became embarrassing.

'Is there any evidence for your theory, Professor Crankshaft?' I queried.

'Most certainly,' cried the great man, wagging his beard. 'Look here, sir. I have been measuring the temperature of the church at numerous and various locations since we first came into the building. You will observe from my notes that the average temperature has fallen by one degree centigrade. The buccal temperature of Mr Fox-Bright, on the other hand, has gone up by an equivalent amount. Our reverend gentleman here is evidently absorbing heat from the air and is directing it towards the organ in a very targeted, purposive way. Unconsciously.'

'Can a difference of one degree produce such large effects?' I asked.

'Oh, my data is only indicative, Dr James. Much more heat transfer might be taking place without its having a sustained effect on Mr Fox-Bright's own body temperature. I should need to take a much more formidable battery of measurements to obtain the complete thermodynamics. However, that is beside the point. My burden is to advise Mr Fox-Bright on what to do. And in fact, I propose two things. First, put yourself on a strict starvation diet for a few days, sir. Second, cool the church down drastically using ice and evaporation. This will deprive your unconscious mind of the energy it needs if it is to attain its ends.'

'And allow Cedric's conscious intentions to prevail?' I asked.

'Exactly,' said the great man.

Crankshaft, eager to help, obtained a large quantity of ice from a manufactory in the City of Norwich, and placed buckets of it around the interior walls of the church. He spent several days taking temperature readings, and finally pronounced that it was time for Cedric to start repairing the organ again.

Astonishingly, Cedric could now mend the bellows without difficulty, restore the fallen organ pipe in its socket, and, with Lord Crankshaft's chauffeur raising the wind, test the keys and the various divisions of pipes. To be sure, the instrument sounded as if it had a bad cold on the chest, but at least it worked. Phrases from Bach, especially those in the bass clef, rippled down the nave, and a few bars of the famous Toccata in D Minor brought the raven to peer through the south windows, fluttering from one to another in an anguish of curiosity and concern.

'Capital!' exclaimed Crankshaft. 'It is as I thought. You have proved the concept, sir, and can now get professional help in the repair of your instrument. I am very pleased. I shall return to London tomorrow and write a paper on this case for the *Proceedings of the Society for Psychophysical Research.*'

***

'He's an old fool', laughed Cedric, pouring me a third glass of port after dinner. 'He's the sort of fellow who believes he can measure and manage everything. Utter nonsense! And my mind is in no sense divided. If anything, Monty, old chap, I'm in danger of becoming quite the monomaniac – my only and my urgent goal in life is to restore this grand instrument to the glory of God, to the delight of the immortal soul of the Lady Henrietta, and to the edification of the holy people of Corpusty. Divided mind, my foot!'

'Oh, come, come, my boy,' I demurred. 'Organ building is a highly technical and expensive business. Are you sure you're quite capable of seeing this thing through?'

'Oh, yes! I shall build such an organ as will open the Gates of Heaven to all who hear it,' cried Cedric, his eyes glistening. 'I'm going to repair the blessèd instrument, and every year, on All Souls Day, I will put on such a Spiritual Concert for the Quick and the Dead that no other village, town or city in Norfolk will have dreamed of before. The most uplifting music imaginable! The dramatic intensity of the Passion story in a toccata! The resigned yearning for Paradise of a tender slumber song! The glory of a three-voiced fugue, its unity in complexity signifying to our feeble minds the inner life of the Most Holy Trinity!'

Mrs Fox-Bright glanced at me nervously.

The lady was evidently uneasy with this kind of talk, as, to be frank, was I.

'Monty,' she said, 'do you really have to go back to Eton so soon?'

'Oh, I'm afraid I must. The Governing Body calls.'

***

Monday 28th October 1929

Every day since my return to Eton, Laetitia Fox-Bright has urged me come back as soon as possible to Corpusty, to help her divert Cedric from his obsessive mission to repair the now infamous organ.

So here I am again, back in Norfolk. I arrived late last night.

But I am afraid that I shall probably disappoint Laetitia. Oh, I have tried to interest Cedric in other things. He and I had a chat after breakfast this morning about the extent to which one can reconstruct the teachings of the Gnostic Valentinus from Irenaeus's account of them in his *Adversus Haereses*, but my young friend soon excused himself and slipped away to St Peter's church, his bicycle very unstable because so heavily laden with wood, metal, leather and felt.

Laetitia tells me that Fox-Bright has been spending whole days in the church, to the utter neglect of his pastoral duties.

***

This afternoon, after I had finished reading Gregory Palamas in the *Patrologia Graeca*, I stepped out of the vicarage, ambled along the Norwich road and sauntered up the hill to St Peter's.

It is not a very steep climb, but it is hard enough for my inefficient heart; and I had to pause for five minutes at the churchyard gate for a rest. As I recovered my breath, Lionel Ember, the churchwarden, approached from the south, sitting on his horse-drawn cart. He waved at me and bade the horse to stop.

'Dr James, if I in't mistaken,' he said.

I nodded, dabbing my brow with a handkerchief.

'Hope you're goin' to bring the vicar back to 'is senses, boy!'

'Has he lost them?'

'Puh!' said Ember, staring at me as if I were in my dotage.

'He reckon he be an organ builder,' said the farmer. 'But what do he know about it?'

'Well, he's a very intelligent fellow, I'll have you know.'

'My foot!' laughed Ember. 'Brains 'as naught to do with it. A job like that, it need years o' solid trainin' afore a man even know how to get goin, boy. And the vicar, well, he be stuck most o' the time. Old Bertie Diggle up Matlask way, he be a true organ builder. Ten years he were, a-learnin' of 'is trade. Well, when the Vicar get too stuck even to pull his boot out o' the mud, he call in Bertie Diggle to rescue 'im. But old Bertie, he get so sick o' the Vicar's botchin' n' bunglin' as he eventually says, "Oh, your reverence, I've gone an' torn a ligament in my leg, and doctor's orders is to be stuck to my sofa, so I can't help you no more." But that ain't true, I know, for I see Bertie a-playing at bowls on Matlask green whenever business takes me round that way.'

'Well, I'm sure Mr Fox-Bright will learn through bitter experience,' I said.

'Aye, bitter,' said Ember, sourly, 'ne'er a truer word!'

He pushed out his mouth and chin in a very judgmental manner, tapped the side of his head with his whip, and drove off.

***

Even before I entered the church, I could hear hammering.

'Oh, hullo, Monty,' said Cedric, emerging into the nave from the tower with a mallet in his hand. 'I was just connecting up the last of the pedal division. If you're happy to wait a little while, you can hear me test it by playing that magnificent pedal passage from old Bach's F Major Toccata.'

'Certainly, I can stay for that,' I murmured.

I carefully lowered myself down onto a chair nearby, still rather fatigued from the climb up the hill. I rubbed my chest as Cedric leapt up the steps to the organ gallery.

'Here we are,' called my friend, turning the pages of the score until he found the passage he wanted. 'Ready, Tommy?'

Tommy Yaxley was an unemployed farm boy whom Cedric was paying a few shillings a day to help with the labour involved in the organ repair, including pumping wind into it as required.

'Right you are, sir,' replied the boy.

The instrument began to wheeze and creak and groan, and then, as Cedric danced his feet up and down the pedal board, an amazing bass-baritone imitation of heavy rain-drops splashing in a deep and muddy puddle erupted from the long wooden pipes housed in the tower.

'I say, that's splendid!' I cried.

I could hear the thudding of Cedric's thick-soled shoes on the pedal board over my head just a fraction of a second before the music burst from the pipes. But then, I noticed, amid these two distinct but correlated patterns of sound, a different type of thud, quite random, but sounding very insistent, an erratic series of dull bangs, that came from somewhere else in the church.

I looked around.

When the music stopped, I felt sure that the bangs were emanating from the chancel. But they too stopped too within two or three seconds of the organ.

'What's that hammering?' I asked.

Cedric looked down from the gallery.

'Oh, not again,' he muttered.

The boy, Tommy, emerged from the tower.

'It must be the crypt,' he said.

'What? You've heard this before?'

Tommy nodded.

'It's probably just an echo of the mechanical action of the organ,' explained Cedric, 'but to make sure, would you mind standing on top of the Kettle vault while I play the organ again, Monty?'

'I say, the floor isn't going to give way beneath me, is it?'

'No, no. Of course not. The flagstones are firmly supported. I'm sure of that.'

I took up my station, a little unwillingly, just in front of the altar.

This time Cedric played the Little Fugue in G Minor. He had not gone beyond the third bar when I felt an insistent hammering beneath my feet. Yes, the very stones were shaking from the impact of blows of some kind from the vault below.

I swallowed rather nervously.

The music stopped.

'Well?' shouted Cedric.

'Definitely some knocking from the crypt,' I called back.

'Tommy,' cried Cedric. 'Bring the crow-bar.'

I could deduce what Cedric's intentions were.

'Are you sure that's wise?'

My young friend did not reply.

I removed myself from the chancel and sat down on another chair.

'I'm sorry,' I said. 'I can't help you. My heart, you know.'

'Of course,' replied Cedric.

I don't know which was more like an excited schoolboy, Cedric or Tommy.

'Come on, guv'nor,' cried Tommy. 'Lever it up here.'

He was pointing to a slight gap between two stones.

Cedric rammed the crow-bar into the gap, and with a great grunt threw all his weight on to it. Tommy placed his foot on the lever and added such weight as he possessed.

After half a minute of intense effort, my two companions raised the stone, manipulated it aside and lowered it down again gently.

Cedric took some matches from his pocket and lighted an oil lamp. Lying down on the floor to the south of the void, he peered with the aid of the flickering light into the dank-smelling gloom.

'Gosh,' he whispered.

'What is it?' cried Tommy, dropping to his knees.

'Two oak coffins,' replied Cedric, 'resting on stone slabs. But one has slid off its plinth and is standing at an angle to the ground, head in the air.'

'Give it 'ere,' cried the boy, seizing the lamp from Fox-Bright's hand.

Tommy jumped down into the crypt.

'It's Her Ladyship what's knocked off her perch,' he announced. 'The coffin's not broke though. It look intact to me.'

'And the other one?' asked Cedric.

'Perfect. Except it's goin' black. Look sort o' scorched. Frost got to it, p'rhaps? No holes though.'

'Maybe we should put Lady Henrietta back on her slab?' mused Cedric.

'If I were you,' I intervened, 'I'd leave things exactly as they are; and for Heaven's sake, seal the vault up again, with as much despatch as you can muster.'

Tommy looked at me with disappointment.

Cedric hesitated.

'Oh, I suppose you're right,' he said, eventually. 'Shouldn't disturb the dead.'

***

That evening, after dinner, Cedric took me into his study to show me a portrait of the Lady Henrietta that hung beside his desk.

He stared at it pensively.

'Beautiful, isn't she?' he said.

'I'm not an expert judge of these things.'

'This was painted just a year before she died, you know.'

'A woman of some character,' I volunteered.

'Oh, undoubtedly. Look at the unflinching gaze of those subtle green eyes, the firmness of the mouth. And yet, the soft hair, the gentle concave nose, those full lips – all very feminine.'

'Not unpleasing to the eye, I can see that,' I admitted.

'She was unwilling to bow to earthly power, being obedient to higher authority.'

This was rather too romantic for my liking.

'And yet,' I pointed out, 'higher authority rewarded her devotion by calling her to its bosom before her four-score-and-seven years on earth were complete.'

Cedric turned and stared at me.

'As Menander says, "Whom the gods love, die young", Monty,' he said, reprovingly.

It occurred to me then – I cannot say why - that Cedric had survived the Great War.

Tuesday 29th October 1929

I stayed in the vicarage today, reading Gregory Palamas again. His doctrine of the distinction between divine essence and energies is most interesting. We feel the effect of the energies, but can know nothing of the essence. How true, of many things!

Cedric was in a cheerful mood when he came back from the church.

'Great progress,' he cried, throwing himself into an armchair by the fire. 'We resealed the conductors and wind chests for the great division today. All those stops now play very well, really. And the key action is remarkably good to say the organ hasn't been maintained for a hundred and fifty years. Only a few loose trackers, which young Tommy and I can put right.'

'We must have a sherry to celebrate,' I suggested.

'What a good idea, Monty,' laughed Cedric.

He went to the drinks cabinet and poured two glasses of Oloroso.

'Here you are,' he said. 'Your good health, old chap. Oh, I have some hazelnuts somewhere too. Let me see.'

Cedric rummaged in the cabinet and produced a bowl of nuts and a curious little squirrel-shaped nutcracker, which he placed on a small table in front of me.

'You know, Monty,' he said, dropping back into his chair, 'I felt rather guilty about leaving the Lady Henrietta's coffin at the slope yesterday. Rather precarious, I thought. So young Tommy and I opened the tomb up again and laid her down with all due reverence on the slab, beside Sir Roger. It seemed the decent thing to do.'

'Oh, did it?'

'Yes, of course it did. And I feel bad that I didn't do it yesterday, actually, because the coffin had been damaged overnight.'

'Really? How?'

'Well, I think it must have slidden sideways, so that the top struck the outer wall of the vault, for the wood of the top left-hand side had been smashed open, revealing the lead coffin inside. The lead itself is a little dented too, but still intact, thankfully.'

'Most distressing,' I observed.

'We put her Ladyship back in supine repose on her slab,' continued Cedric, 'so it should all be stable now. No more accidents, eh?'

'Quite.'

'I can only imagine that it's the vibrations from the longer flue pipes that are shaking the coffin around.'

'But Sir Roger's hasn't moved, has it? I queried.'

'No, not at all. Strange that, what?'

'Perhaps his is heavier. Harder to move?'

'I'm sure Lord Crankshaft would say it was all down to resonance,' said Cedric.

'You mean the Lady Henrietta's coffin resonates with certain organ notes, while Sir Roger's doesn't?'

'Yes. Something like that. I'm no scientist though!'

***

Wednesday 30th October 1929

Remained at the vicarage again, reading Palamas.

Had a sandwich with Laetitia Fox-Bright at one o' clock. She then went up the hill to take a pork pie and some lemonade to Cedric and young Tommy. I sat before the fire and dozed.

Awakened at about two by the sound of the front door banging.

Copious weeping in the hall. Laetitia *tristis*, plainly.

I went out to offer such consolation as I could muster.

'My dear, whatever is the matter?'

'Oh, Monty!' wailed my hostess. 'Cedric is becoming obsessed.'

'There, there,' I said consolingly, pressing the fluid eyes to my waistcoat.

How I hate the dampness of a shirt.

'When I went into the church, Cedric was in the organ loft, playing a voluntary of some kind. I'm afraid I know nothing of music. All I know is that the organ was thundering away, and Cedric kept turning around, while he played, to look down the church towards the altar.

'Of course, I glanced down there too.

'The Kettle crypt was open again. Young Tommy Yaxley was on his knees by the void, staring intently into the depths. Then he looked up, his face full of excitement, and raised up a thumb to Cedric in the gallery.

'Cedric must have pulled out even more stops at that point, for the organ blasted out chords far louder than I had imagined possible.

'"What are you doing?" I cried, but neither of them could hear me.

'Neither of them could see me either, though I was there in plain sight. They were both wrapped up in the excitement of whatever macabre plan it was that they were executing.

"I strode down the aisle to the chancel.

'It was then that I noticed a raven, fluttering against the outside of the great east window over the altar, pecking at the glass and screeching in alarm.

'"What on earth are you doing, young Yaxley," I said to the boy, as sternly as I could.

'But he didn't hear me, or look up at me, even though I was standing beside him.

'His attention was still focused on the contents of the crypt.

'Of course, I looked down too.

'You won't believe this Monty, but as the music roared out, the lead of Lady Henrietta's coffin broke open just above her head, and began to peel back slightly of its own accord – as if someone were opening a tin of luncheon meat! God help me, I couldn't move my eyes. I watched, Monty, as great locks of the Lady's auburn hair became visible in the gap.

'Well, I screamed. Oh, did I scream! But still Tommy ignored me.

'Or didn't even hear me!

'They were doing some sort of macabre experiment, Monty. I'm sure of it.'

***

Thursday 31st October 1929

By the time I came down for breakfast, Fox-Bright had already left for the church.

Laetitia treated me to more sogginess of face and spirit.

'Speak to him, Monty. Please. He'll listen to you.'

'Well, really,' I said. 'I'm not sure that I'm able to.'

'What do you mean?'

'He won't listen. Even if I can find the right words.'

'Please. He respects no-one more than he does you.'

'Oh, very well, then.'

I was grudging and churlish, I'm sorry to record.

I had to climb that damnable hill again. I'm sure it is taking a month off my life every time I go up it. The air is misty and damp too, and that isn't good for my lungs. I had to spend five minutes coughing and leaning heavily on my stick at the churchyard gate. That attracted the attention of the raven, which flew over and began to strafe me. What does that perishing bird want?

I shuffled my way slowly into the church. As I went through the porch, the bird took up its sombre station by the first of the south-facing windows, and watched me silently through the clear glass as, once inside, I painfully made my way to the altar.

The church seemed to be empty, but I could hear voices.

Oh, yes. I knew who they were, and where they were.

Cedric and Tommy, in the Kettle crypt.

Damn them.

They hadn't heard me, so I surprised them, bending over the face of Lady Henrietta.

'What the Devil do you think you're doing?' I demanded.

'Christ!' swore the boy, for which offence his vicar, rather unfairly, I thought, clipped him around the ear.

'Gosh, you startled us, Monty,' called up Cedric, emolliently.

'Will you leave that poor woman's remains alone?' I cried.

'But look here, Monty, something quite miraculous is happening,' protested Cedric.

'Miraculous?' I repeated. 'Miraculous?'

'Well, I think so,' argued Fox-Bright. 'It's not Tommy and I who are opening up her coffin. It just happens of its own accord. And look at the Lady's face. It's as if she died an hour ago. It's the organ, I'm sure of it.'

'Whatever do you mean?'

I sighed helplessly. I had to lean on my stick to stop myself from falling into the hole.

'There's a correlation here,' explained Cedric. 'As the organ becomes more functional, so the cadaver becomes more lifelike. I'm sure of it. She seemed – sort of withered – pale and fragile like old thin paper, the other day. But look at her now! The redness of the lips, the smoothness and plumpness of the skin. The beauty of the hands folded on her breast. Look for yourself, man. Look!'

'For Heaven's sake!' I shouted. 'Cover the woman up!'

'Look,' shouted Tommy. 'She's breathin'! I see her chest move!'

'Don't be ridiculous,' I snapped.

'Haven't you noticed?' asked Fox-Bright. 'The air is fresh down here. There is absolutely no odour of corruption.'

'But that's only because the place is so very dry,' I said. 'Good drainage, at the top of a hill, for God's sake!'

'Well, she enjoy the music, do Her Ladyship,' opined young Tommy. 'That's what's makin' 'er all plump and shapely again, in't it? I'll bet them membranes an' bones in 'er ears are all a-vibratin' like new.'

'My dear boy,' I said, as condescendingly as I could, 'the Lady Henrietta is now in a place where the bones of her ears will make not the slightest difference to her happiness, I assure you!'

'You're wrong, Monty,' replied Fox-Bright. 'Something marvellous is happening here, but I don't quite know what it is yet. Let's seal the tomb up, Tommy, and get the church ready for All Saints tomorrow. We can resume our explorations the day after.'

***

Friday 1st November 1929 - All Saints

Fox-Bright did at least have the decorum to seal the crypt.

Nothing of any great significance happened while I was in the church today, apart, of course, from the solemn celebration of Holy Communion. The ten or so people who belong to the Church Visible in this parish joined *spiritually* with their ancestors in the Church Invisible, in the worship of Almighty God.

The organ was serviceable, but only Fox-Bright could play it. I couldn't.

'You play the piano, Monty,' he had said to me, before the service. 'You do it.'

'Quite out of the question. The organ and the piano are totally different instruments.'

I could see that the man was vexed, but I would not budge.

The service was in the evening, and it was dark. After the final Amen, Cedric had to dash from the altar, candle in hand, and climb the stairs to the organ gallery, to play the voluntary.

Of course, by the time he started, most of the congregation had left.

Bach's Gigue in G Major. Very jaunty.

But by Heaven, it did not suit my mood.

***

Saturday 2nd November 1929 - All Souls

'Do you have a service today too?' I asked Fox-Bright, over breakfast.

'No, I just say private prayers,' he replied.

I gazed at him.

'I suppose it's a particularly important day for you personally,' I murmured.

He reddened slightly, and looked at his boots.

'Indeed, Monty. I lost a lot of friends, you know.'

'Young men, full of life,' I said.

'Man that is born of woman hath but a short time to live, and is full of misery,' intoned the man whom I had looked upon as a protégé. 'He cometh up and is cut down like a flower; he flieth as it were a shadow, and never continueth in one stay.'

'Are you spending the day in church again?' asked Laetitia, in a strained way.

'Yes. I must.'

'You could at least have the decency to send that young boy away,' cried the wife.

'He enjoys our work in the church,' said Cedric. 'And it gives him an income.'

'It's unhealthy!' cried Laetitia. 'Morbid!'

Fox-Bright rose from the table and left the room without a further word.

***

The sky was clear but the wind was highly disconcerting.

From the window of the living room of Corpusty vicarage, I could see tiles blowing off the roof of the old seventeenth-century watermill over the road and splashing down in the river.

'Goodness,' I said to Laetitia, who was sewing by the fire.

'It's very rough,' she replied, not looking up.

I sat myself down in the armchair on the other side of the hearth.

'Hark to the howling in the chimney!'

'Yes,' she replied. '"The wind bloweth where it listeth, and thou hearest the sound thereof, but canst not tell whence it cometh, and whither it goeth."'

'Very apposite. But this is a westerly gale, I think.'

There was a sudden roar of wind and a silver birch in the grounds of the Mill House opposite toppled over and crashed into a wall. Bricks flew everywhere.

Laetitia and I went up to the window for a better view.

'This isn't safe,' she said, as plant pots flew before our eyes.

'No, better move away from the glass,' I agreed.

We had just resumed our seats when over the howling of the gale we both heard the distinct clang of the great bell in Corpusty church tower, amid all the other shrieks and wails of the accelerating air.

We looked at one another sharply.

'Why would Cedric be ringing the big bell now?' asked Laetitia.

'I don't know, but I don't propose to go out in this furore to discover the reason,' I said.

'No, quite.'

I lighted my pipe and picked up the *Patrologia*.

Laetitia resumed her sewing.

***

I was dreaming about John Milton kissing Satan when I heard Laetitia scream.

I opened my eyes and saw Cedric Fox-Bright standing in front of the vicarage fire, shaking and shivering, blood trickling down his face from a nasty gash on his forehead.

'Cedric,' I cried. 'What's happened?'

Fox-Bright began to sob.

'It's my fault,' he moaned. 'Mine alone.'

'Good God, man!' I expostulated.

'Where's Tommy Yaxley?' asked Laetitia.

Cedric fixed his eyes on the carpet and would not look up, even when I rose and shook him firmly by the arms.

'I wanted to see the changes myself,' muttered Cedric. 'In the Lady Henrietta. Tommy was always the first to see them, and that wasn't right, was it? This was my project. He was just the helper. So, I taught him how to play a few chords on the organ, how to use the stops and couplers, and the swell box. Then I set him going, playing the same phrases over and over again, while I watched in the crypt with a storm lantern so that I could see in minute detail what the effects were on the Lady's body.'

'You're insane,' muttered Laetitia.

'No, I'm too sane,' countered her husband. 'How I wish I weren't. And let me tell you, when young Tommy pressed his foot on the swell pedal and opened those wooden slats to the glory of God, such beautiful strong chords burst forth from the organ that I had not heard before; and the Lady Henrietta opened her equally beautiful dappled green eyes and gazed with curiosity on my own face. It's the truth! I did not imagine it!'

'Oh, Cedric!' wailed my friend's wife.

I for my part kept quiet.

'The Lady's lips parted as if she were preparing to speak,' continued Cedric, 'but before she could do so, a tremendous crash and rumble and clatter came from the west end of the church; the organ music turned to a cacophonous set of wails; and the flesh of the Lady's face crumbled away before my very eyes, turning to fleshy scraps and greasy dust and grey bone.

'I yelled at this and clambered out of that crypt as rapidly as my legs could move. Which wasn't fast enough, I can tell you. The stench of decay is in my nostrils still, despite staggering home amid the fury of this damnable hurricane.'

'But what happened at the tower end?' I pressed Cedric. 'We heard the bell toll.'

Cedric looked from one to the other of us in silence.

'The force of the wind on the tower,' he said. 'It must have been that. It made the stonework move, causing the bells to come crashing down, all three of them. The organ's ruined, Monty. Just so much scrap metal and a multitude of matchsticks. After all that work. After restoring the Lady Henrietta to her rightful glory. Ruined!'

This fellow with a Military Cross began to sob quietly.

'And Tommy,' said Laetitia, rising to her feet. 'Where is he?'

Cedric gazed at his wife, and then at me.

'Dead,' he said.

We sat in silence, all of us, for what seemed like minutes, but can't have been.

'He was in the organ gallery,' continued Fox-Bright, eventually. 'When the bells fell, the gallery went down too, and poor Tommy was crushed to death by stones dropping from the tower arch. I don't know how I'm going to find the strength to repair the organ again.'

Laetitia became very pale at these words.

She rose from her chair and slapped her husband's face with the back of her right hand.

***

Wednesday 2nd November 1932 – All Souls

I have been back to Corpusty to visit Laetitia Fox-Bright, who still lives there, though Cedric does not. In fact, he has disappeared. Nobody knows where he is.

Apparently, Cedric wished to have Tommy buried in the crypt with the object of their shared obsession, but it proved impossible to lever up the slabs again. Every time the men from Ember's farm tried, the crow-bars would snap. The boy was eventually buried in a corner of the churchyard, in a spot overlooking the Bure valley, to his parents' great relief, with a holly bush planted over his breast for company.

The organ was sold for scrap. The parish made little money from it.

Laetitia tells me that Cedric Fox-Bright wept uncontrollably at these outcomes. He became fearful and despondent, and neglected his parish duties terribly.

I had a sad interview today with the churchwarden, Lionel Ember.

'People don't care to go in the church, boy. It's scarcely used now. Even though we repaired the tower, just so as to stop it fallin' down, like. The air can be foul in there, in the church. Aye, a sort of a dead smell. But we done what we had to do, and shored up the walls and tower, and made the place decent by cementing up them coffins in the crypt so no interferin' types could go a-pokin' around down there again.'

'Quite right too,' I said, warmly. 'But tell me, Mr Ember. If the organ's been played, as it has, what happens to the money from the Kettle Trust now? Surely, the Covenant's been broken? Don't all payments stop?'

Ember laughed at me.

'Oh, bless you,' he said, 'there ain't hardly any money left. All them properties whose rents mainly funded it were near cliff tops in places like Overstrand, Sidestrand and Trimingham; and after the Great Storm o' 1929, they all fell into the North Sea one by one, all washed away by the incessant poundings o' waves on them crumbly cliffs. All gone, sir. Lost for ever!'

***

Editor's Note

I was curious, naturally, about the fate of Cedric Fox-Bright, after editing this story from Dr James's papers, and I therefore made enquiries into his movements after leaving Corpusty.

The only definite information I could find was a Death Certificate, which showed that on All Souls Day, 1940, the Reverend Cedric Fox-Bright was found in the churchyard of St Thomas, Friarmere, high on the Pennine hills in what was then the West Riding of Yorkshire, frozen to death.

This information led me in turn to a short news report in the *Oldham Evening Chronicle*, which reported that Mr Fox-Bright was found with his arms raised and crossed in front of his face, on which was grimly fixed a look of the utmost horror.

THE ISLAND OF TYSKÄR

Monday 7th September 1908

One of the more disagreeable aspects of being a head of house is that one is called upon from time to time to adjudicate in dreary disputes among the dons of other colleges. I have just returned, ear-battered and stiff-limbed, from policing an outbreak of the *furor academicus* at All Angels College.

It was, I suppose, a solemn task - but, to be frank, I had the utmost difficulty in stopping myself from shrieking out loud with laughter. My goodness! The bitter pomp of the one disputant, the gleeful invective of the other!

No, judicial gravity is not for me.

It was, of course, a case of Age versus Youth.

The plaintiff was Dr Ernest McWatt, a distinguished but dull chap who is Corbel Professor of Holy Scripture and one of the most senior Fellows of All Angels. Professor McWatt accused the defendant of bringing his beloved college into disrepute through at best scholarly incompetence and at worst utter charlatanism.

The defendant was a lively young sprite, a handsome boy, one Alban Ivory, clothed with a very distinguished First - but not yet a Master of Arts - who had had the temerity (in his accuser's view) to argue that the Apostle Paul was not the humble tent-maker of pious legend but in fact a member of the Herodian royal family. To be exact, young Ivory alleges that Saul, to use the Apostle's Hebrew name, was a first cousin of King Herod Agrippa I of Judaea.

Utterly affronted by this (in fact, rather interesting) notion, Professor McWatt had tabled a motion before the Governing Body to have Ivory expelled from the Fellowship to which he had only just been appointed. Ivory responded by accusing McWatt of being a blinkered horse with a love of plodding in closed circles of ever decreasing radius.

The Provost of All Angels, Admiral Sir Andrew Colander, called me in to arbitrate. Sir Andrew is an old chum of mine from my undergraduate days, when he was naval equerry to my friend Prince Eddy, that is to say, more formally, Prince Albert Victor, the oldest – but now sadly deceased – son of our present King, at Trinity College. Colander was a valuable companion on punting expeditions on the Cam, but was also a serious naval historian with many a salty yarn on the tip of his tongue.

Now, I don't like McWatt. He is one of those grim-faced, blue-chinned, grey-eyed men who know only one kind of flower and condemn all the others as weeds. Think of Holbein's portrait of the studious Erasmus in profile, minus the great scholar's gentle hint of an ironic smile. Quite dreadful.

Ivory, on the other hand, is charming, and though perhaps a little too interested in exotic flora, is willing to test whether they truly belong to the garden of scholarship.

Personally, I don't think Ivory's argument that Paul was a Herodian stands up. True, Paul is keen not to provoke the Roman authorities and indeed to collaborate with them, and this was certainly a trait of the Sadducees and the Herodians, who owed not only their thrones but the high priesthood in Jerusalem to the permission of Rome. And Paul's references to earning his living as a tentmaker do have a ring of condescension about them, as if this were not his natural milieu. But the 'facts' offered in evidence by Ivory are dubious. The mention by Paul in the Epistle to the Romans of 'Herodion, my kinsman' is quite obscure. Most importantly, there is no independent proof that the 'Saulus' who is mentioned as a politically active member of the royal family, and as a kinsman of Agrippa, in Josephus's *Antiquities of the Jews* is the same chap as our Apostle.

There is equally no compelling reason to think that the Epaphroditus whom Paul refers to as his 'companion in labour, and fellow soldier' in the Epistle to the Philippians is the Epaphroditus who was the private secretary of the Emperor Domitian. On the other hand, the mention in the Book of Acts of a plot in Jerusalem, in which forty men took an oath not to eat or drink until they had killed Paul, does suggest that the Zealots saw him as an enemy. But I think that the Gentile author of Acts is confused about the relationship of the Sanhedrin to the high priesthood; and in the want of more and *better* evidence, Ivory's theory must be regarded, in my opinion, as not proven.

McWatt, however, takes Ivory's arguments to be an insult to Sacred Scripture.

As I sat listening to them argue in the Council Room at All Angels, I could see in the older man's eyes the light of an unearthly fire: a pale, cold, flickering; not warm, but penetrating and chilling; dissecting rather than healing, judging rather than reconciling.

As a man who has spent many years studying the Apocrypha of the New Testament, I am too familiar with the disturbing, strange and sometimes absurd content of the pseudepigraphical texts to take McWatt's highly conservative position seriously. Compared with, say, the unedifying nonsense in the so-called Infancy Gospels of Christ - in which the child Jesus withers up the son of Annas the scribe like a dead tree for dispersing a pool of water that he had made, Ivory's position on St Paul's royal status is at least respectable - and quite possibly true.

At the Hearing, I therefore ruled in Ivory's favour - and opined that though the young fellow had not proven his scholarly argument to my own satisfaction, he was nevertheless engaging in serious work.

McWatt immediately rose from his chair with all the bulk and menace of an anvil-headed cumulonimbus cloud. My word! Bolts of lightning sparked from his eyes, rumbling growls emerged from his chest and mouth.

'You, Montague Rhodes James,' he cried, pointing an accusing finger at me, 'are a disgrace to your venerable father, who is a respectable clergyman of sound evangelical views.'

McWatt then spun on his heel to face Ivory.

'And this puppy has befouled himself,' he added, with an ugly sneer.

Ivory's skin turned a delicate blue-white, a red flush curving beneath each eye-socket, his eyes intense and staring, pupils dilated to an extent that I found disconcerting.

Tuesday 8th September 1908

This morning I received a letter from McWatt attacking me for being 'ethically incompetent'.

McWatt regards himself as an expert on moral theology. He has spent most of his academic life vigorously attacking the teachings of the Roman Catholic saint, Alphonsus Liguori - a bishop in the south of Italy, who died in 1787 - a man who believed in giving the struggling faithful a little bit of slack - and contrasting them unfavourably with the writings of the contemporaneous Anglican divine, William Law, who in the degree of his great influence on the earnest-minded and in the clarity of his prose is what McWatt himself would like to be.

I think there is a lot to be said for the *via media* in all things, myself. There is nothing to be said for the *odium theologicum*.

I felt a little sorry for Ivory, so I invited him to the Lodge for tea today. He turned up with a gift for me, a charming early edition of Tasso's *Gerusalemme Liberata*, which reminded me very much of one with the poet's autograph that I had coveted at a shop in the Charing Cross Road in the late '70s. I hesitated to accept it, in the interests of neutrality, but reflected that to a man so rich it was but a trifle.

Ivory noticed my pianoforte and asked if he might play.

'Yes, something cheerful,' I replied.

But what he played was – beyond a certain initial brilliance – passionate, indignant, vehement; full of dark feelings, half-disguised as light.

'Good Lord,' I said, when he had finished. 'What was that?'

'Haydn. The sonata in B Minor,' he replied. 'A sullen and querulous key, don't you think?'

'Indeed!'

I lighted my pipe thoughtfully.

'Full of yearning and frustration, I should say.'

There was a pause; then Ivory said, 'He is out to get me, Dr James.'

'McWatt?'

'He won't accept your judgement. I'm sure of that.'

Thursday 10th September 1908

I was at the Master's Lodge at All Angels today, taking tea with Admiral Colander.

'I can't thank you enough, Monty, for dealing with that squabble among the theologians. Talk about angels on a pinhead, eh?'

'Quite,' I said. 'I'm all for tradition, but we also have to understand its complement, the stream of ideas against which the tradition defines itself, and changes, and grows.'

'Exactly,' said Sir Andrew. 'Broad minds keep us balanced, what?'

'I'm curious to know what you think of these new *Dreadnought* battleships, Admiral?'

'Splendid inventions,' cried my old friend. 'Fisher, the First Sea Lord, is an odd chap in many ways, but he's spot-on with this design – big 12-inch guns, big steam turbines – the Germans are in a blue funk to catch up with us, but they won't - we've got another six a-building already!'

The Admiral threw back his head and laughed immoderately.

But he was interrupted by a hailstorm of knocks on the door.

'Enter,' called Colander.

Jenkins, the head porter, stepped inside, cap in hand, moustache twitching.

'Terrible news, Sir Andrew,' he cried.

'Well? What is it?'

'Professor McWatt is dead, sir.'

'Great Scott,' ejaculated my friend, jumping to his feet. 'Why? How?'

'He appears to have been crushed by a bookcase, sir. Fractured skull, I should think, but then again, I'm not a medical man, sir.'

'An accident?'

'Possibly, sir, but there are reports of a heated argument taking place in the room just prior to a loud crash and bang being heard.'

'Heard? Heard by whom?'

'The chaplain, sir, Dr Potter, across the landing.'

'But an argument with whom, Jenkins?'

The porter coughed and glanced at me.

'With Mr Ivory, sir.'

'Oh dear. I say, that sounds bad. Don't you think so, Monty?'

I nodded, dreading what was about to unfold.

'And where is Mr Ivory now?' continued the Master.

'He appears to have fled the college, sir.'

'Great Scott! I think you'd better call the police, Jenkins.'

'I've already taken the liberty of doing so, Admiral.'

***

The first thing I saw was the pool of blood on the polished floorboards. It was soaking into the Turkish rug at one end, and slowly dripping down through a small knot-hole at the other. The man who lived in the set below would soon notice an unpleasant stain on his ceiling.

Professor McWatt's head was lying partly on the rug, partly on the boards, resting on its side, the lifeless eyes staring towards the empty grate in the fireplace; the right temple and cheek bone appeared to have been directly shattered by the top and uppermost shelves of the book case, which still lay across the poor fellow's head.

I could not help but notice that a valuable 1559 edition John Calvin's *Institutio Christianae Religionis* lay in the pool of blood, its pages darkened by the increasingly viscous liquid. Several volumes of Charles Spurgeon's sermons also lay scattered around the sanguine shore.

'I really hope that this was an accident,' growled the Admiral.

'Surely, the bookcase was secured to the wall?' I queried.

'Just a couple of screws, by the looks of it. See here, holes in the wall where the wooden plugs have pulled away completely,' replied Sir Andrew.

'Some considerable force must have been applied to the book case to do that.'

'Or the plugs had just become loose with time,' sighed my friend. 'Best not to touch anything. The police inspector will curse us if we wreck his trail of clues, what?'

***

I cannot make up my mind whether there has been foul play at All Angels or not. What has quickly become evident is that Ivory has vanished completely.

Ivory's college rooms, when we inspected them, afforded us only one clue as to his state of mind - and one that is, I think, rather hard to interpret in the absence of other evidence.

A volume lay open on his desk. It was the *Summa Theologiae* of St Thomas Aquinas, Part the First, showing Aquinas's Question 114 – The Assault of the Demons. Heavily underscored was this passage:

Sed contra est quod apostolus dicit, ad Ephes. VI, quod non est nobis colluctatio adversus carnem et sanguinem, sed adversus principes et potestates, adversus mundi rectores tenebrarum harum, contra spiritualia nequitiae in caelestibus.

'Well, my Latin isn't up to translating that,' grunted the Admiral.

'No matter,' I said, reassuringly. 'I shouldn't know how to plot a course for the Grand Harbour at Valetta either. Let me translate. "On the contrary, The Apostle says (in Ephesians 6:12): 'Our wrestling is not against flesh and blood; but against Principalities and Powers, against the rulers of the world of this darkness, against the spirits of wickedness in the high places.""'

'Very sinister,' remarked the Admiral.

'Perhaps,' I replied. 'But we have no idea why Ivory was reading this, or when.'

'Oh, yes we do,' said Sir Andrew.

'Eh?'

He pointed to a tiny fleck of still moist blood at the top of the right corner of the page.

'Gosh!' I cried. 'We must mention that to the constabulary.'

We looked through the other rooms in the set. The chest of drawers in Ivory's bedroom indicated a hurried withdrawal of clothes, but all else was in order.

The police could find no further clues either when they arrived shortly afterwards.

Monday 14th September 1908

The burial of Professor Ernest McWatt took place in the antechamber of All Angels' Chapel this morning. As directed by the Corbel Professor's last Will & Testament, we sang Charles Wesley's hymn, *And can it be that I should gain / An interest in the Saviour's blood?*

The singing was not quite lusty enough in my view. That hymn really requires a vigorous Non-conformist congregation from the North of England, not an anaemic choir like that of All Angels.

McWatt's unfinished manuscript, *Exposition of the Words of the Prophet Jeremiah*, was buried with him, at the request of his widow.

Wednesday 23rd September 1908

Extraordinary. I was shaving this morning in my bedroom, taking great care not to nick the skin in the crease between my bottom lip and chin, when, at the very left edge of the mirror, I suddenly noticed the livid face of Ernest McWatt peering at me from behind.

I did not care to turn around, but stared at the glass. My heart began to palpitate.

'What the Devil do you want?' I cried, quite involuntarily.

But the image disappeared with my question.

The only frowning face in the room was mine.

Monday 2nd November 1908

All Souls Day.

Naturally, I have thought tenderly all day of my dear mother, lying in her grave at Livermere. How I miss her. May she rest in peace.

I returned from chapel this evening feeling full of grace. What a marvellous rendition one of our choir boys, Nathanael Elkins, gave of Handel's great aria, *I know that my Redeemer liveth*. It was utterly perfect.

This mood of serene contentment was, however, quickly destroyed by my discovery that someone had been riffling through my personal letters in the old bureau in my bedroom.

The bureau was definitely locked when I left for Divine Service. When I returned from dinner, I found it not only unlocked and open, but my correspondence strewn over the carpet all around it. This is bizarre. There is only one key to the desk, and I keep it in my pocket. Also, the Lodge itself is always locked when I am elsewhere, and the senior porter on duty has the only other key.

The letters were all face down on the floor apart from three which I had received from young Alban Ivory before his disappearance. These three – which were of no great consequence, I have to say; they merely passed on Ivory's impressions of that curious old church of Saint-Bertrand-de-Comminges, high in the French Pyrenees – these three were tightly crumpled up.

There was also a strange odour in the room.

A dank, unpleasant smell.

Friday 25th December 1908

It is now – what? – two o' clock in the morning. I have had a particularly convivial evening with several friends. The port was especially good. Arthur Benson gave me a splendid present - a fine blend of Syrian latakia and Macedonian yenidje tobaccos, with a Cavendish base - which I have just smoked in my favourite cherrywood: such freshness of flavour.

As I review the year since last Christmas, I cannot help but reflect on that strange business of Alban Ivory and Ernest McWatt. Ivory has not been seen again – not in his college, nor anywhere else in Cambridge, nor by his sophisticated friends in London. His family, who live in a grand mansion somewhere down in Devonshire, have made anxious enquiries among their various cadet branches - but these too have been equally fruitless.

I can only imagine that Ivory, feeling morally guilty of McWatt's death, or perhaps fearing (I suspect, an unjust) conviction in a criminal court, has sought refuge in some remote corner of His Majesty's Empire - or possibly even in the United States, which, Benson tells me, offers even more obscure hiding places.

I find it difficult to believe that Ivory intended deliberately to kill the Corbel Professor, but I suspect that I shall not know the end of this odd tale before I give up the ghost myself.

Friday 1st January 1909

I did not stay up to see in the New Year but went to bed just after ten. I felt rather weary from a day spent making detailed comparisons between Bonnet's Greek text of the Acts of Thomas and the Syriac as given by Wright and Mrs Lewis. I do not doubt that for the most part, the Greek of our current manuscripts is translated from the Syriac; the frequent stiffness of the Greek is testimony to that; but the literary quality of the Greek in the Martyrdom passage is so good that I can only think that this has been independently preserved from a Hellenic original and added back into the translation from the Syriac.

The strangest thing has happened!

An hour ago, I ate a light breakfast that Mr Clegg from the Buttery had kindly left out for me the night before, and then I went for a stroll around Front Court. I returned to my study, and, sitting down at my desk, I found lying upon it, to my surprise, a copy – that I had jotted down on a scrap of paper on a visit to Sweden in 1901 - of a contract in his own blood that a theological student, Daniel Salthenius, had made with the Devil at Uppsala University in 1718. This contract actually bound the Infernal One to provide the impecunious student with a bottomless bag of money in return for the latter's body and soul.

The young fellow was denounced by his parents, I believe, and sentenced to death by the local authorities - but escaped. He later converted to Pietism, much to the disgust of the Orthodox Lutherans, who tried unsuccessfully to hang the Devil's contract around his neck again. Salthenius eventually became professor of theology at Königsberg, where he eventually died possessed of a magnificent library of 22,000 volumes.

His library is only partly catalogued to this day.

But the question is - how did my scribbled copy of Daniel Salthenius's diabolical contract get to be out on my desk? Frankly, I do not know. I think - but I am not entirely sure - that it was secreted in a travel case at the bottom of the large wardrobe in my bedroom.

There is also a sort of greenish thumb-print on the copy. I cannot brush or wipe it off. It seems to be stained into the fabric of the paper somehow. It is as manifest on the back as on the front.

Thursday 1ˢᵗ April 1909

I love the Scandinavian countries. Imagine, then, the delight I felt when by the second post today I received a letter from the Librarian of Gripsholm Castle, in the Södermanland region of Sweden, asking me to go and spend some of the summer there cataloguing a newly discovered trove of royal manuscripts. These documents are mostly about King Gustav I Vasa's decision to appoint bishops independently of Rome, and include letters from the Persson brothers, Olof and Lars, to the newly Protestant King, advocating Lutheran dogma and hymns & promoting their translations of the Mass and of the New Testament into common Swedish.

Very generously, Dr Bergquist, the Librarian of Gripsholm, which is still a royal palace though one seldom used nowadays by the Sovereign, has said that he can arrange and pay for accommodation at a nearby inn – not only for myself but also for one friend, if I should like to take along a travelling companion with me.

I think it would be good to have a chum to smoke with in the evenings, and I am going to ask Sir Andrew Colander, who has been a good friend of mine ever since our undergraduate days - and of whom I have been seeing much more since that strange business between Messrs McWatt & Ivory - to accompany me.

I do not know who is funding this project. Presumably, it is either His Majesty King Gustav V in person, or his government. I must ask Dr Bergquist about this.

I also cannot help but wonder whether there is a connection between this invitation and the sudden appearance on my desk a few months ago of Daniel Salthenius's devilish contract. I suspect that sometimes there may be an occult and non-causal relationship between events, such that one calls forth another as a kind of echo, whether before or after the main event. We must not take time too literally, perhaps?

In this case, Dr Bergquist's intention to invite me to Sweden might have summoned up the note I made years ago of the Swede Salthenius's bargain with the Devil, ahead of his actually sending me his kind letter.

But even if this true, how did the thing get from my wardrobe to my desk? This is certainly a mystery - but I do not intend to let it spoil my fun at Gripsholm.

Monday 5th April 1909

I have wired Dr Bergquist to say that the Admiral and I will pitch up at Mariefred, the town beside which Gripsholm Castle stands, on Monday 3rd May - for a stay of up to four weeks. We shall take the boat train to Harwich, the North Sea ferry, the railway via Hamburg to Stockholm, and then the slow & tortuous boat journey along Lake Mälaren to Mariefred.

Tuesday 4th May 1909

Dr Bergquist – what a kindly old fellow, thick white hair, bushy moustache, gold-rimmed spectacles gleaming in the light of his desk lamp. A smile of some great degree of curvature always plays upon his gentle features.

'I really cannot say who is paying for your services, Dr James,' he said, in response to my curious questioning. 'I do not know myself. I received a letter saying that a ... sufficiency ... had been deposited in a bank account by an anonymous donor for me to collect in person.'

'How much?' asked the Admiral.

'Oh, I cannot tell you,' laughed Dr Bergquist, a trifle nervously. 'It is a lot. You can afford to stay in our excellent inn here at Mariefred for several years, I think!'

My commissioner was seated behind his large desk in the magnificent royal library. All around us were leather-bound volumes of the works of the Fathers, from Clement of Rome to Augustine of Hippo, from Justin Martyr to Maximus the Confessor, as well as worldly works such as Machiavelli's *Prince* and *Discourses*, and, from a wholly different perspective, the civilising tome *De Jure Belli ac Pacis* of the Dutch jurist Hugo Grotius.

These volumes suggested to me that we were in the comfortable old lair of sovereigns who liked to rule the souls and not just the sinews of men. I glanced at the portrait of His Majesty King Gustav I Vasa above the fireplace. Such a large bulk; a staring face, quite hard; fiery red hair and broad beard, both severely square-cut; a glove already removed from his right hand, as if in readiness to slap an idle courtier, or perhaps seize a sword in wrath.

'As you will have noticed, the castle is now mainly an art gallery and museum,' said Dr Bergquist. 'But we do have the manuscript collection about the Reformation – which has not properly been catalogued at all – which we should like to see put in good order.'

'Yes,' I said, and pointed at a painting hanging on the wall.

'Isn't that John Calvin?'

Our Librarian glanced over to where I was pointing.

He squirmed rather.

'Yes, yes,' he said. 'It is very polemical, of course.'

The portrait showed Calvin's nose rotting on his face. Green worms wriggled out of what was left of his nostrils. The worms were decorated with diabolical red dots.

The Admiral guffawed heartily.

'These theologians!' he cried. 'They're more vicious than a Company of Marines!'

'Gentlemen, gentlemen,' protested Dr Bergquist, growing rubicund.

'Oh, don't mind me,' said the Admiral, suppressing, not very well, a grin.

'Sweden is now a very tolerant and peaceful place,' pointed out the Librarian. 'And we can keep it that way if we understand better the conflicts that erupted with the Great Reformation.'

I nodded.

'Which,' continued our host, 'is why I'm so glad that this anonymous benefactor has enabled us to ask you to catalogue the papers of King Gustav the First Vasa, Dr James. But now I should take you to your lodgings so that you can relax a little after your long journey.'

***

'Oh, yes, that was a violent time, gentlemen,' said Gustaf, the portly and jovial landlord of the Mariefred Inn. 'I am so glad that we do not live in a time of bitterness and conflict.'

Gustaf's inn stood on Kyrkogaten, very close to the town's handsome white church, the tall clock tower and elegant arcaded steeple of which had a certain modest dignity. From the back of the premises, his guests could also enjoy a grand view of Lake Mälaren and of Gripsholm Castle commanding Mariefred bay.

Gustaf took us up a crooked staircase and showed us our rooms. They were quaint with their gently undulating floors, but pleasantly decorated and, I need hardly say, spotlessly clean.

'What a splendid vista,' cried the Admiral, looking out from my window.

'What is that little island half a mile or so from the castle?' I asked.

'Oh, that is the island of Tyskär,' said Dr Bergquist.

'It is a very holy place,' added Gustaf. 'Saint Katarina lived there as a hermit before she became the Abbess of Vadstena. It is said that she sent the Devil flying into the lake through the sheer power of her prayers, and the Evil One – well, he did not like getting wet!'

'Is that a church I can see on it?'

'It is a small chapel,' answered Dr Bergquist. 'The one built by Saint Katarina. We make a pilgrimage there once a year, on the saint's birthday. Otherwise, we leave the place alone, as a place of peace and quiet for the angels and the birds of the air.'

He smiled happily.

Thursday 6th May 1909

The manuscript collection of Gripsholm is kept not in the Library itself but in a high room in the south-eastern tower. Warmed by the sun, cooled by the breeze, well away from the water, this is one of the best places in the castle for storing parchments and papers. The documents are kept in good strong boxes stored in cupboards, the boxes affording protection from light, insects and rodents.

Today, among the many letters to and from the Persson brothers, I came across one from Gustav Eriksson Trolle, the last Roman Catholic Archbishop of Uppsala, who in 1521, during the Swedish War of Liberation and associated Protestant Reformation, was forced to flee to the safety of the Danish court at Copenhagen. Trolle's letter (to the Lutheran theologian Olof Persson) was a bitter complaint about 'heaven on earth being destroyed by ignorant men'. This 'heaven on earth' was in fact the Island of Tyskär that Gustaf described to us yesterday.

I can see the island very clearly from the window by which I am working. It is a small place - a narrow strand, a few rocks, a patch of vegetation on higher ground on which stands the tiny - and by now somewhat decayed - stone chapel. Saint Katarina Ulfsdotter created in that chapel 'a place of such sanctity that every type of demon is repelled from the island and can in no wise enter thereupon', according to this epistle.

'And who was she?' This Ulfsdotter woman?' asked the Admiral, when I read Trolle's letter out to him, later.

'Oh, the daughter of St Birgitta Bigersdotter,' I replied. 'Birgitta was a mystic, who founded the Bridgetine Order. Her daughter was perhaps a little more practical, and wrote a devotional manual, *Siælinna tröst*, that is to say in English, *On the Consolation of the Soul*.

'She also accompanied her mother on a pilgrimage to the Holy Land. On the death of Birgitta in 1373, Katarina brought the old lady's body back to Sweden for burial at the Abbey of Vadstena on Lake Vättern. That last service for her mother being accomplished, Katarina came here to Lake Mälaren and created a hermitage for herself on that tiny island of Tyskär over yonder. There she fought and vanquished the Devil, making the island a place of luminous sanctity. Purified by this experience, Katarina returned a year later to Vadstena and became the Abbess of the Bridgetines.'

'Remarkable woman,' pronounced Sir Andrew, nodding his head thoughtfully. 'She'd have made an excellent lighthouse keeper, what?'

Friday 7th May 1909

This evening, after a day reading the thoughts of Olof Persson on the Lutheran doctrine of consubstantiation, I sat and relaxed on a lakeside bench in front of the Castle, smoking in my comfortable old briar the last of that heavenly tobacco blend that Arthur Benson had given me for Christmas.

The air was still warm. There was only a gentle intermittent breeze. As I gazed out over the water, I noticed a golden light glinting every now and then on Tyskär. It showed very clearly because the eastern sky behind it was pale and darkling. The light seemed to come from the ruins of the Bridgetine chapel that had been abandoned since the Reformation. The light was flashing like a signal because, in the breeze, the boughs of trees moved back and forth in front of the shrine.

I noticed a rowing boat coming from Tyskär, low in the water, and making a beeline, or so it seemed to me, for the very bench on which I was sitting.

As this vessel neared the shore, the rower, who faced the stern to give the boat motive force, stopped rowing, turned around, and gazed at me.

I beheld – I thought - the wan face of Alban Ivory.

Anxious and *fearful* - these words hardly register what I saw on that face.

The face scrutinised my own, presumably for signs of emotion. And yet, I could see that I was not its sole focus of its attention. Rather, it glanced nervously from side to side and, by repeated strokes of the oars, seemed to want to move the boat back to Tyskär.

'Colander,' I cried, leaping to my feet. 'Colander. Come here at once!'

'Eh?' said the Admiral, removing a Havana cigar from his mouth. He had been entertaining himself by blowing smoke rings around a budding red rose. 'What is it, my dear fellow?'

'Look,' I whispered, pointing over the water.

Sir Andrew turned and peered towards the island.

'What do you mean? Can't see anything, myself.'

'Good Lord! Well, he was there, a moment ago, rowing towards me.'

'Who was?'

'Alban Ivory... I think.'

'Impossible. There's not a boat in sight, Monty. Must have been a squadron of low flying ducks, or something of the sort. Your eyesight's never really been up to much, old man.'

Saturday 8th May 1909

I dreamed last night that I was at the water's edge again, that night was falling rapidly and that Alban Ivory was rowing towards me in a boat illuminated by blazing torches. I wakened in a cold sweat and had to get up and smoke a pipe.

There was something ominous about the dream. Oppressive.

I could not help but think that the figure of Ivory was some kind of psychopomp, come to ferry me to an Isle of the Dead.

But had I really seen Ivory? I hardly think so. Why, then, am I having such strange dreams, waking – it seems, from my earlier experience - and sleeping?

It's all quite absurd. Ivory is alive. I'm pretty sure of that. He has, I suspect, adopted a new persona as a schoolmaster in some obscure township of Queensland or other out-of-the-way place in the farthest reaches of the Empire where he can evade Official Enquiries.

My bizarre experiences are – I think - an attempt by my *dreaming* mind to draw something to the attention of my *waking* mind. But what?

I can only conclude that my dreaming mind is grossly inefficient.

Sunday 9th May 1909

I had such a shock this morning.

I rose at seven. The first thing I did was raise the blind in one of the windows, put on my spectacles and stare at the Island of Tyskär. Its every lineament was clear in the sharp easterly light from the already high sun.

The place looked innocent. I smiled at my own fears.

I poured water into the bowl and washed my hands, face and chest. The air was still quite cool at this time, so I dried myself very vigorously with the larger of the two towels provided. I put on clean underclothes from my travelling case and then turned to get my tweed suit from the wardrobe.

I opened the wardrobe door and put my hand inside.

Something wet grabbed my hand, and enclosed slimy fingers around it.

I emitted a scream. I am embarrassed to record the fact, but that is what I did.

I had to look inside.

What I saw nearly made me vomit into the wardrobe.

Hanging there, within my suit, was the decaying corpse of Ernest McWatt. The pitiable face gawped at me from near the hook, the flesh rotten but the impress of the heavy bookcase very obvious still in the bones of the face and skull. A bloody left hand was clamped around my shaking right hand. I saw a rib or two peeping through the waistcoat. From the bottom of the trousers, two bony and scarcely articulated feet protruded.

'Angels and ministers of grace …,' I muttered, and crumpled to the floor.

I awoke some minutes later to find Admiral Colander and the landlord kneeling beside me, tipping repeated doses of brandy into my mouth.

I spluttered, spat out the last of the burning liquid and cried, 'The wardrobe! The wardrobe!'

'What about it?' said Sir Andrew.

'I saw …'

'You saw what?'

'My suit.'

'Eh? Your suit frightened you?'

'Did you see what was in it?' I gasped.

'Well, I'm not in the habit of going through a fellow's pockets, Monty.'

I sat up and stared at my suit.

Of course, it was unoccupied by any body, alive or dead, and was perfectly clean.

'I think I must have been sleep walking,' I said.

'Oh,' smiled the landlord. 'A nightmare, eh?'

'Yes, yes, that must be it,' I said.

I felt as nervous and powerless as a frightened boy at that point.

And I made a point later of going to High Mass at the village church.

Monday 10th May 1909

I quizzed Dr Bergquist about the island of Tyskär.

'Is it an Isle of the Dead?' I asked.

'No, no,' he replied, with a laugh. 'It has never been used as a place for burials. But it has had the reputation of being a very sacred place ever since Saint Katarina lived there in the fourteenth century. And to be fair, her heart is *said* to be buried there. But even if that is true, she is the only person of whom part is buried there. The island is regarded as a holy place, and people do not go there often. That does not prevent the birds from flying there, of course. For them, it is a sanctuary too. And a very comfortable one, judging from the number that flock there.'

'I thought I saw lights on the island on Friday evening,' I said.

'Really?'

'Yes. And I noticed a chap in a boat rowing towards the Castle, who can only have come from the island.'

'Devout people do go there sometimes. It is a quiet place to pray.'

'I thought this was someone I knew.'

'That would be a remarkable coincidence.'

Indeed. Another strange coincidence that occurred today – though I blush to record it, even in my own notebook – was that when I visited the privy chamber at the inn after dinner, I found a copy of William Law's *Serious Call to a Devout and Holy Life* propped up against the wall beside the porcelain.

The book was in English, and bound in excellent leather. I opened it. It had clearly been well read, judging from the discoloration of the top right corners. I searched the endpapers and found a manuscript note: *Ex libris Ernest John Porteous McWatt.*

I immediately felt the blood draining from my brain. I benched myself on the lavatory lid, closed my eyes, and uttered a short prayer for help.

I examined the book afresh. Was this an hallucination as the invasion of my suit had been? Minutes passed, and the book still felt solid and firm in my hands - weighty, leathery, papery. I opened it at random, and yes, the contents made sense – well, at least grammatically - as to the purport, I am not a man for great solemnity – on every page I inspected.

Once I had completed my ablutions, I left and took the book with me.

Admiral Colander was smoking one of his robust cigars in the lounge. I handed him the volume I had just found and asked him what he made of it.

'A work of divinity,' he said, 'printed in London in the year 1832. A handsome book. I say, it belonged to that blighter Ernest McWatt. Did you know that, Monty?'

'I found it in the lavatory.'

'How bizarre. Who put it there, I wonder?'

I shrugged my shoulders.

'Well, it isn't the ghost of McWatt,' insisted Sir Andrew. 'Someone is trying to break down your nervous system for some obtuse reason.'

He drew heavily on his cigar and blew a fragrant cloud above my head.

'I can think of two possible culprits,' he continued. 'One is Dr Bergquist. I rule him out on the grounds that's he's a bit of an Emily Jane. The other is Alban Ivory, who, I strongly suspect, is hiding somewhere in this vicinity and who wishes to trifle with you for obscure reasons of his own. He paid for you to come here. That's obvious, isn't it? He's trifling with you for his own ends, inducing hallucinations like the one you had yesterday morning. The fellow's putting opium in your porridge, I should think. And I dare say that he stole this book from McWatt's library and is now using that to alarm you too.'

'But why should he be so malevolent? He was never a vicious man,' I protested.

The Admiral shrugged his shoulders.

'Perhaps the fellow's a maniac,' he suggested. 'Killed McWatt deliberately. I should watch out if I were you.'

'Really, Andrew! I can't believe that I've been *that* wrong about his character!'

'Well, you can never tell with these highly-strung types. Had a chaplain once - when I was captain of *HMS Victoria* – well, the blessed fellow threw a gunnery lieutenant overboard for whistling *A bicycle made for two*. Extraordinary!'

We subsided into silence.

'I think,' I said, eventually, 'that we should pay a visit to the Island of Tyskär.'

'Splendid idea,' replied the Admiral. 'I'll row you out there.'

Tuesday 11th May 1909

I stood in front of Gripsholm this morning and gazed out towards Tyskär. Shielding my eyes from the climbing sun, I scanned the island for signs of life.

My eyesight is not good, and I could make very little out at such a distance; but I believe that standing on the shore of that holy island was Mr Alban Ivory, staring back at me.

I am inclined to think that Ivory *is* hiding out there – but from what? Well, I have my suspicions, of course, but I did not want to state them explicitly just then to my old friend Colander. Merely alluding to them in the vaguest terms provoked something of a rant.

'Suspicions!' he cried. 'It's a racing certainty, old man. He killed McWatt on purpose! And I'm prepared to bet a very large sum that he paid for you to come here too.'

I felt obliged to pick up the *non sequitur* in the Admiral's thinking.

'Why on earth would he have paid for me to come here, if he's hiding from Justice?'

'Don't underestimate the blighter's cockiness. He's snubbing his nose at us.'

'Well, let's leave that on one side for now. Will you row me out to Tyskär, Admiral?'

'Of course, I will. By God, I wish I were in my own county! I could issue a warrant for his arrest, if I were. Damn it all, I am a Justice of the Peace, you know!'

I laughed.

'You're not in your own country, let alone county!'

***

Ivory was standing on a little stony beach, waiting for us.

He smiled at me weakly, like the sun on a wintry day.

'You've got to help me, Monty,' he murmured.

'Why?' demanded the Admiral, stowing the blades.

'"He prowleth around as a roaring lion, seeking whom he may devour."'

Colander look at Ivory with intense suspicion on every feature of his face.

'Who is "he"?' he asked – not that he had any need to. Deliberately obtuse.

'I've tried lots of places,' continued Ivory, ignoring Sir Andrew. 'Glastonbury, Lindisfarne, Mont Saint Michel, the Castel Saint Angelo, Mount Athos, Mount Tabor, Mount Sinai. They all work for a while, but eventually I have to flee again. And I'm so tired of that, Monty. *This* place is losing its power to protect me now too.'

'Protect? Protect?' growled Colander.

'I'm an innocent man,' replied Ivory, calmly. 'McWatt's death was an accident. True, I wanted to throw his books down, to show my contempt for his so-called scholarship. But I didn't mean to kill him. Not at all.'

Ivory ushered us over to the tiny chapel of Saint Katarina, which had walls and a roof, but no glass in its three windows or door in its entrance. A few branches of fir trees were strewn over the floor as a sort of carpet or, maybe, a bed. At the eastern end of the building there was a small rough-hewn altar of stone, with a few spent candles sitting rather forlornly on top. Through the east window behind, I could see the sun now rising high over Mälaren.

'I don't know what I can do to help you,' I shrugged.

'I want you to conduct an exorcism,' said Ivory.

'But I'm not a priest.'

'You're a devout man, in your distinctive way, full of innocent joy; that's enough.'

I smiled.

'You wish to expel the malevolent spirit of Dr McWatt?'

'Something like that.'

I hesitated.

Ivory placed his hands heavily on my shoulders. They were as cold as an Arctic wind. Their touch bit through my coat, shirt, skin, flesh and sinew down to the very bone.

The air was calm outside, but in my breast, I could feel a tempest rising.

I nodded my consent.

My teeth suddenly chattered uncontrollably, my limbs quivered with nervous tension. I felt as if I might any moment be sick over the rug of firs.

'Be quick,' urged Ivory.

I ransacked my memory for any sacred words that might be apposite.

'Put on the whole armour of God, that you may be able to stand against the wiles of the devil,' I began. 'Resist the devil, and he will flee from you. Come out of this man, O unclean spirit.'

Nothing obvious happened as a result of this rather Protestant approach. I therefore tried some of the words associated with St Benedict of Nursia's Medal as a Papist alternative.

'Nunquam Draco sit tibi Dux!' I cried.

This attempt to banish the lordship of the dragon also failed.

'Vade retro Satana!'

Ivory raised his eyebrows hopefully at this last pronouncement, but after a few moments began to look disappointed again.

I decided to try the original Greek from Saint Matthew's Gospel.

'Ύπαγε όπισω μου, Σατανα!' I yelled.

I felt not a little ridiculous, as if I were self-consciously play-acting again, like the student thespian I had been many years ago in Aristophanes' comedy, *The Birds*.

As I spoke, I waved my right arm loosely towards the waters of the lake, which is where I took the brooding spirit of McWatt to be located. But I kept my eyes always firmly on Ivory.

To my astonishment, Ivory himself began to fade away before my eyes, like an image made fleetingly on the condensation of one's own breath on a cold window.

There was on the young man's face – what? A smile of triumph, perhaps – maybe of relief - but also a grin, with derision in it – gloating – an admixture of contempt.

Something was wrong here.

I heard howls of dismay from the water. It was Ernest McWatt's voice that I could hear, making frenzied circles of sound around the Island of Tyskär on the wind.

Gazing at the place where, but a few moments before, Ivory had been standing, I could see only a collection of faint fragmentary patches of flesh tones, whites, and pinkness.

'Good luck, Monty, you silly old fool,' came the boy's whisper.

The grin on his red lips was the last thing to dissolve into motes of dust.

Cheshire cat!

Silence.

'What the devil just happened?' asked the Admiral, eventually.

'I thought I was exorcising Professor McWatt, but I seemed to have exorcised Ivory instead.'

'Eh?'

***

Mälaren looks beautiful but is actually full of filth. The towns that stand beside it have since the beginning of civilization been in the habit of discharging their raw sewage into its waters. In high summer, the stench along the shoreline is an olfactory reminder of Hell.

Admiral Colander launched our dinghy back onto this ocean of effluent.

My old friend applied himself vigorously to the rowing, and we made rapid progress back to the jetty at Gripsholm Castle from which we had begun our journey.

But the closer we came to the jetty, the more the wind veered round and pushed us against our will - and against Colander's muscular effort - back towards the deeper water. The wind howled, and alongside its screaming I thought I could hear the dark and dismal voice of Ernest McWatt roaring insanely the name 'Alphonsus Liguori, Alphonsus Liguori, Alphonsus Liguori.'

I do not know why I said it, for I am not of the Roman persuasion, and have no inclination towards it, but I found myself crying out the words, 'Alphonsus Liguori, protect us!'

At once, the wind dropped.

But this was *not* good for Admiral Colander.

He had been squatting as low as he could in the boat, consistent with being able to operate the oars, and had been getting some purchase by leaning with all his weight against the sheer force of the offshore wind. But as soon as the wind dropped, the starboard oar leaped out of its rowlock and struck him forcibly on the chest. He tumbled backwards against the gunwale. In the blink of an eye, he had toppled over into the water.

Opening his mouth to yell, Colander could not but swallow a mouthful of the lake.

How vigorously he spat out the residue.

I helped him to clamber back aboard, with distaste, for, to be frank, he stank.

Back in Mariefred, our host Gustaf insisted that Sir Andrew take off his clothes in the yard, and threw several buckets of cold water over his quite naked body. Only then did he allow the Admiral to wrap himself up in a towel and go indoors for a hot bath.

'I know the risk,' muttered Sir Andrew. 'Typhoid. A real danger.'

When he reached his lavatory, Colander opened his mouth, pressed two fingers down his throat and vomited into the bowl.

'That should help,' he said.

I held my handkerchief to my face.

'Now Monty, be a good chap and get me a large brandy, will you?'

Upon my return from the restaurant, Colander swallowed the spirit in a second in the belief that its sudden arrival in his stomach might sterilise it. Then he threw me out and soaked in a hot bath for thirty minutes.

Exhausted, we ate dinner, and retired early.

Thursday 13th May 1909

The Admiral is complaining of a headache.

I left Colander sipping tea at the inn while I went to Gripsholm and made notes on the records of Olof Persson's treason trial of 1540. I rather suspect that his real crime was to be no respecter of persons and that he did not fear to criticise his King. Of course, he was found guilty and sentenced to death. I saw in the State Papers how his friends managed to secure a Royal Pardon for him two years later, namely, by continually praising his immense labour in translating the whole of the Bible into the Swedish tongue.

I pondered on how even Persson's own brother Lars, the Lutheran Archbishop of Uppsala, had been prepared to sign – did actually sign, in his own hand - Olof's death warrant.

Saturday 15th May 1909

Colander's own words are the best index of his condition, I think.

'I feel damnably weak.'

'Close the window, will you, my cough will wake the dead in the churchyard.'

'Open the window now, I feel too hot.'

'Good Lord, get me a towel, Monty. Nosebleed.'

The doctor says, 'Yes, it looks like typhoid fever, but it's too early to be sure.' Colander certainly looks febrile. His face is flushed. He perspires constantly.

The poor fellow's eyes are always searching the shadows in the corners of the room.

'What are you looking for?' I asked.

'Cassocks,' he replied.

Good light was streaming in from the room's three south-facing windows, but I lighted Colander's oil lamp and placed it in one shady angle and fetched the lamp from my room for another dim recess.

'Bless you, Monty,' sighed my friend.

He relaxed. Seemed to settle into relatively peaceful sleep.

Wednesday 19th May 1909

'The brute's laughing at me. Over there. Stop talking foreign nonsense, damn you.'

Colander and I are the only people in the room.

'Sit up, and drink some water,' I said.

But he can't raise himself from the bed at all.

'Never slaves,' muttered the Admiral, just now. 'NEVER!'

He seems to be arguing with some imaginary interlocutor.

He's fallen into a fitful sleep again.

Thursday 20th May 1909

'It is as I feared,' whispered the doctor. 'See here, Herr James, these rose spots on the chest are typical. I can also hear rattling noises in the bronchi, which is another sign, I'm afraid.'

He put the stethoscope back in his Gladstone bag.

I could not help but remember that Mr Gladstone had resigned the Premiership over his Cabinet's insistence on building more battleships. Financial profligacy, he said.

'Splendid orator,' Sir Andrew used to say of the Grand Old Man, 'but dangerously reluctant to give the Other Fellow a bloody nose when necessary.'

'Except with words,' I would reply.

'Sometimes only gunfire will do, Monty.'

I shuddered, recalling this conversation, seated on the rickety chair by my friend's bed.

'I can't bloody move, Monty,' murmured Colander.

'Be still, old man. Rest is good for you.'

'Hell, my guts! They're killing me.'

'You have pain?'

'Yes, damn it.'

I rose and called the doctor up from the restaurant downstairs.

The doctor palpated my friend's stomach.

'What's that damnable row?' demanded Colander.

'Your digestive system,' said the medic.

I put a handkerchief to my nose.

'Monty, you might want to clear out. Don't want to disgust you.'

The doctor nodded, picking up the bed pan.

But I needed the handkerchief even in the corridor, and on the stairs.

Friday 21st May 1909

'Shut up!' cried Colander.

The words were firm, the voice flabby.

'Who are you talking to, old man?'

'Him. Old grim jaw.'

'Only you and I are in the room, Andrew.'

'Listen.'

I kept the vigil that my friend had enjoined upon me; and I heard a low, malicious voice whisper, from the corner of the room by the door, the words of the Chronicler: 'And after all this, the Lord smote him in the bowels with an incurable disease.'

I leaped up and pulled open the door.

'Jehoram indeed,' I muttered, indignantly.

The corridor was empty, but I thought I heard a snort on the stairs.

From behind me, Colander cried, 'Ye gods, I'm on fire!'

I returned to the bedside.

'Shadrach, Mesech and Abednego knew nothing,' muttered the Admiral.

'Pneumonia,' whispered the doctor. 'He is very ill.'

I nodded.

'Is there anyone you should notify in England?'

'All Angels.'

The Swede looked at me curiously.

'His college, in Cambridge,' I explained.

Monday 31st May 1909

Colander's face is grey and blue.

His breathing, infrequent though it now is, is dreadful to listen to. What he is feeling himself, I do not know. Is he aware of anything by now?

He coughs up blood, bloody sputum.

He groans, and lays an emaciated hand on his chest.

I wipe his brow. Will the cool water will harm him?

It will.

Tuesday 1st June 1909

The moon is waxing gibbous. It sends a pale clear light over the churchyard, which, as I look out from the window of the staircase, appears peaceful – and eerie.

It is always the shadows that disturb me. Can there be light without shadow? I think not. We might try to compress the darkness, or expel it to wild places that are totally beyond our brightly lit lives, but no - we can never suppress it completely.

And here, tonight, in Mariefred, in the dim south-eastern corner between church tower and nave, I think I see the outline of a tall man in a cassock. There is a hint of grey hair reflecting the moon's pewter rays.

Somewhere in the churchyard, an invisible dog is barking.

I must send a cable to Colander's poor wife.

Widow.

Monday 21st June 1909

I have been to the Midsummer Feast at All Angels College.

As is customary at All Angels at this Time of Light, those of us in Hall drank one after the other from the Loving Cup in memory of the Faithful Departed. Inwardly, I gave thanks for the now extinguished life on earth of my old friend, that vibrant fellow, Vice Admiral Sir Andrew Colander, Knight Commander of the Most Honourable Order of the Bath.

After dinner, we retired to the Senior Combination Room for port, brandy and cigars. I took out my favourite old briar and began to fill it with good Dutch *Troost* from my pouch.

I gradually became aware that someone was playing the Haydn B Minor Piano Sonata in the Large Parlour next door. 'Surely, Ivory can't be here?'

I strode across the Combination Room and flung open the Parlour door as one of those crashing chords let loose a dark flurry of frenzied semiquavers.

A saturnine young man played at the piano. It was not Ivory. How could it be? I had seen Ivory's image dissolve before my own eyes, like so many layers of paint being peeled away from a canvas.

The pianist looked at me curiously as I stared at him, but did not cease from playing.

I turned tail and wandered over to the chapel. It was still unlocked. I took the pipe from my mouth and pushed open the oaken door. In the half-light of the antechamber, I looked down at the fresh marble grave-slab of my poor friend Sir Andrew Colander. He had been interred, unsatisfactorily in my view, beside Professor Ernest John Porteous McWatt.

Thursday 24th June 1909.

Lady Colander came to see me today at the Lodge.

'The Senior Tutor at All Angels telephoned me this morning,' she said, 'to say that the remains of a young man have been found in the cellar of the bath-house at the back of the college. The police inspector in charge says that they are, in all probability, those of Alban Ivory.'

'But how could they know?'

'From papers found in his coat pocket, I believe, but also from his height and build and a few other physical traces that still remain.'

'How gruesome. He must by now be ... well, I hardly need to say it. Have they been able to establish a date of death? A cause?'

'They believe that he died on the day that Ernest McWatt was killed last year.'

'The 10th September?'

Lady Colander nodded.

'Ivory had an unclipped railway ticket of the same date in his pocket, for a journey from Cambridge to Plymouth; and the pathologist says that the extent of the decay of the corpse – oh, do forgive me, Monty ....'

'By his own hand, do you think?'

Her Ladyship paused.

'I couldn't say. His head was immersed in an old wash-tub of water, I believe.'

Now I paused.

'And the rest of him?'

'Kneeling.'

I could not help but think of the look of triumph and relief I had seen on Ivory's face on the Island of Tyskär when I finally pronounced those efficient words of exorcism.

Sunday 31st October 1909

Sometimes, in the quiet of the night, I hear in my room the sound of a snort of contempt from Professor McWatt's well-rotted nostrils; the full horrors of which are, by some mercy, ever hidden from my sight by dark shadows, no matter how bright my lamp might be.

THE BONES OF PASTON

Tuesday 12th September 1899

I've been working at Peterhouse for a couple of days now on a descriptive catalogue of the manuscripts in the Perne Library.

I like the Perne, perched as it is with its ancient leather-bound volumes over the modern thoroughfare of Trumpington Street. It affords us the best example in England of a medieval library. Peterhouse is, after all, the oldest of the Cambridge colleges, founded in 1284. Oxford has a few colleges of slightly older date; but their manuscript collections do not radiate quite the same degree of glory.

What currently interests me most in the Perne, though, is a rather eccentric document I discovered there today.

I had just finished taking notes on the early 15th century manuscript, *Robertus Lincolniensis Doctrina Cordis*, and was turning my attention to the *Tabula Super Sermones Augustini*, when, at the back of the cabinet, I discovered a much more recent document, made of linen fibre, and written in fairly modern black ink, entitled *A Record of the Bizarre Experiences of William Bodkin, Scholar of St Peter's College, upon the Death of Y^e 2nd Earl of Yarmouth*.

A manuscript with such a title could not fail to pique my curiosity.

The thing had evidently been written by this chap Bodkin himself on Thursday 15th January 1733, just after the start of Lent Term. But who, I wondered, was the second Earl of Yarmouth?

I consulted *Burke's Peerage* and saw that the peer in question, one William Paston, had died on Christmas Day 1732, aged seventy-eighty, and without issue. The earldom had thus become extinct.

This William was the last of the main line of the Paston family, of Norfolk, seated most recently at Oxnead Hall near Aylsham, but emanating originally from the village of Paston, situated on the sea-coast some twenty-five miles or so north-west of from Great Yarmouth. In their giddy rise as landowners, lawyers and courtiers, roughly from the year 1400 until the last breath of the Royalist second Earl, the Pastons had produced a huge quantity of letters on family and public business, of an importance to historians of the late middle ages and early modern period that I should find it difficult to exaggerate.

But back to Bodkin. I append his manuscript here:-

In the evening of this day, the Fifteenth of January of the Year of Our Lord 1733, I, William Bodkin, Scholar of St Peter's College in the University of Cambridge, was sitting in my rooms, on the first floor by the Buttery Stairs, in Old Court, reading my Greek Testament by the light of a good lamp, when I chanced to look up, and saw standing before me a man in the Antique costume of some three hundred years past, namely, a very high black sugar loaf hat, a blue doublet and a long green over-gown of a yellow floral pattern. The Time was between the 9th hour of ye chapel clock and the 10th.

The man, who was by visage some fifty years of age, gazed upon my countenance with stern eyes and fixed mouth, making no motion to speak. It being Winter, I had a small fire burning in the grate, and my strange visitor, standing between it and me, occluded both its light and warmth; which was but Natural.

Unnatural, however, was a grey light - like unto that of a moonbeam - which shone from the fellow's Face. Upon noticing this, my flesh grew Chill, and I gathered my blanket close around me. As the fellow still spake no word, I said unto him, trying the while not to let a quiver sound in my voice, 'Pray, good sir, who art thou?'

The man moved his hands aside as if to shew the quality of his raiment, but this signified Naught to me. A long silence ensued, the apparition's eyes rolling up and down, hither and thither, full - it seemed to me - of Anguish.

I was pondering whether I must needs speak a second time myself, when the apparition slowly opened its strangely pale lips and mouth.

A sound reached my ears like unto the East wind blowing across the Fens, carrying upon it the faint words of a person too far distant to see. These words were like so many sighs; not easily could I understand them; but their purport was thus:

'I once had mine own abode in these Rooms,' said the ghost, for that was surely what it was that stood before me, 'and I made study of ye law here by the light of yon window. Of Inner Temple was I next; and a Knight of the Shire for Norfolk, and aye, a Justice of the Peace; and many Acres of land did I own, many broad acres.'

'Yes, sir,' replied I, 'but your name, sir?'

'John Paston, of Paston town,' said he. 'I took my leave of this crazy-cracked and fickle World in the Year of our Lord Fourteen-Hundred and Sixty-Six, in the City of London, and my corpse made its slow journey back to Norfolk escorted by twelve torch-bearers on a great hearse as rightly befitted my Dignity. I had secured me a place of burial in the Quire of Bromholm Priory in the parish next unto Paston, that of Baketon, which Priory is the blessèd possessor of a Relique of the True & Most Holy Cross, which should keep me, thought I, from the Terrible Pains of Purgatory.

'I had me fourteen men a-ringing of the passing bell at Bromholm, to fend off the rabble of wicked shrieking Demons who would cast my poor corpse as bait to entice their Lord the Devil to fish fiendishly for my Free Soul; and I disbursed many Pounds of Gold for a Feast *in memoriam* of my poor Self at which my Folk and Friends made glad with forty barrels of beer and ale, as many gallons of fine red wine; aye, and more poultry, meat, eggs, milk, cream and goodly baked bread than any other family in these parts of England hath ever imagined for a funeral feast.'

'I wish I'd been there,' I remarked.

The spectral fellow held up an admonitory hand-palm.

'More weight of beeswax than of a brawny man in the heaviest armour was used to make a great candle - higher than the Tower of Babel itself - to burn for weeks over my grave,' he continued. 'And of Charity, many pounds of good coin were dispensed to the alms-seekers of Paston and Baketon to shew the love and care I had for my poor brothers and sisters in Christ.'

'Truly, a magnificent event, sir,' I said. 'Why then do you not rest in peace, but rather disturb mine?'

The shimmering figure groaned like the east wind in a Cambridge chimney.

'My sleep,' said he, 'was perfect for Seventy Years, a restful slumber, awaiting the sound of the Heavenly Trump and the raising of the Dead into the Air; aye, a sleep made perfect by my Sure Knowledge, at the moment of passing out of this Wicked World into the Realm of Shades, that I would rest next beside the Most Holy Cross of Bromholm. But oh, good sir youth, my soul was rudely awakened from its hope-filled slumbers by the Raucous Voice of a devil, one Richard Layton, and his capering imp, Sir Thomas Legh, commissioners of a sacrilegious King, the Eighth named Henry, who rudely ordered the Priory to be pulled down over my bones and my very Tomb destroyed.

'Good sir, I wailed over my Ruined Sepulchre until I saw my grandson, Sir William de Paston, retrieve the remnants of my Bones from the sacred soil, and carry them unto the church of St Margaret at the town of Paston, where he interred them afresh in the chancel thereof.

'And that, good sir, is where my Mortal Remains yet rest.

'Every year, I have shewn myself to Sir William and his descendants in the male line, to command each and every one of These my Lawful Heirs to restore my bones to their rightful place in the ruined Quire of Bromholm, which was and ever will be sanctified by the True Cross, though that Great and Holy Relique of our Saviour has been taken and abused by the Beast, as the demons delight in shrieking in my ear without Cease. And so, my fellow Petrean, I beseech thee, deliver my bones unto Bromholm, that ere long I might rest again in Peace.'

'Sir,' I replied, 'as a Christian gentleman, I wish you well in your endeavour; but what you speak of is rank Popery, and not to my taste.'

'I beg thee by the bowels of our Saviour, sir, assist me, please.'

'No. It would be sacrilege to disturb the soil of a church.'

The apparition gazed at me uncertainly.

'Good gentle man,' it whispered, leaning toward me in a confiding manner, 'I know of a great treasure hidden in darkness in Norfolk. A most heavenly treasure. If thou shouldst be so fine as to restore my bones to Bromholm, I shall reveal unto thee the whereabouts of such gold and silver as will be a more than just recompense for your kind care.'

I hesitated to accept this bribe, but reflected on how I could put the gold to good use in scholarly and religious pursuits more appropriate to our Enlightened Age.

'Very well,' said I, 'I shall do as you request. But you must swear an oath that you will indeed reveal the whereabouts of this hoard to me.'

'By St Peter's beard, I shall of a certainty reveal it to you, my friend,' cried the spectre.

And with those words, he vanished.

Signed : *William Bodkin*

Pinned to this paper was another one of later but unspecified date, a copy of which I also add here:

In this memorandum I give the sequel to the events of ye 15th inst.

I was sure that I had not merely dreamt the Apparition, but had seen some Spirit that was not of mine own mind's inventing. I therefore went on the following Monday (ye 19th) to my bank and took therefrom four guineas.

I next procured me a place on the coach to Norwich. Arriving there, I took another going unto the market town of North Walsham.

At Walsham I rested the night in ye King's Arms and the next morning recruited an idle boy to shew me the way by foot to the village of Paston. This entailed a tramp of some four miles by lane and field.

'Where is the parsonage?' I asked the youth.

'Don't rightly know,' said he. 'Look for t' second biggest crib, I reckon that be it.'

After near enough an hour of searching, we found the Rectory on a horseshoe-shaped lane a little way from the church. I hammered on the oaken door. It opened after a minute to reveal a short old man with a bald dome of a pate soaring above a narrow fringe of thin white hair, his spectacles perched upon an aquiline nose. In his left hand he held a copy of Lucretius's *De Rerum Natura*, in the Latin.

'Good sir,' said I. 'Do I have the honour of addressing the Rector of Paston?'

'You do, young man,' said he. 'I am the Reverend Mr Jones. May I assist you in some way?'

'Well,' I answered, 'I am an undergraduate of Cambridge University, interested in the story of ye famous Paston family, whose letters shed a wondrous light upon the shadows of their lives and cares in those long defunct olden days.'

'Indeed, they do.'

'Pray, sir, would your Reverence be kind enough to shew me the whereabouts of the Remains of that John Paston whose bones first lay in the Priory of Bromholm?'

'Why, yes, the John Paston who died in 1466 is now buried in the chancel, here at St Margaret's, at the southern side of the altar,' said the priest. 'Come, I'll shew thee.'

The grave was a table tomb of indistinct markings, but which must once have borne, I think, the Paston Arms - as some of the other tombs still did.

When Mr Jones shewed me the tomb, the Lad I had employed as my Guide whistled uncouthly and said, 'So the old boi's bones lie unner here do they?'

I cuffed the rogue for his impudence.

'Aye,' answered the vicar, a kindlier soul than I. 'But under the soil, of course.'

The Boy looked disappointed. I believe he had hoped to smash open the Tomb there & then and find a grinning skull beneath, fixing him with its vacancy of eye.

I muttered to the parson: 'I was hoping to make detailed drawings of the tombs, but the light fades. Is there an inn nearby where I might stay?'

The old man seemed discomfited by my question.

'Well,' said he, 'a walk of two miles or so will take you to the fine village of Mundesley, where I dare say some fisherman's wife could make you a bed. Or, you could reach North Walsham before dark if you set off now. But you are welcome to sleep in my back room if you don't mind a hard bed and a small fire. Your boy could make himself a berth in the hay of my barn, with a warm stone from the kitchen range to keep him from freezing in the small hours.'

'Well, that is handsome of you, sir,' I cried, pressing his hand. 'I am of course willing to recompense you for any victuals that we eat.'

I took several shillings from my pouch. The Rector beamed upon them happily.

'Well, in that case,' said he, 'I shall bring up a bottle of claret from my cellar.'

'And port, if you have it,' I cried, producing another shilling.

My object was to get the good man to doze as quickly as possible so that the Boy and I could go and dig up John Paston's bones from the church chancel in peace. We made a heavy dinner of Cold Pig's Face, Mustard, Hard Cheese, Bread, Butter and the remainder of a Fruit Cake that the reverend gentleman produced from his larder; and the old man, quite overcome by the repast and the wines, repaired to a settee near the dining room fire. As soon as he had tumbled so low into the arms of Morpheus that he snored with all the regularity of a Pendulum Clock, I indicated to the Boy with a jerk of my thumb that we should leave for the church.

Noticing a key in the dining room door, I wondered whether to lock the Clergyman in, so that if he woke, he would be unable to lock us out; but decided not to. Were the old man to discover our Absence, I should simply invent some excuse for it. In the meantime, I added a couple of logs to the fire in hope that this might prolong his Slumbers.

I did, however, take his kitchen door key with me.

In the Reverend Gentleman's barn, we found a spade and some strong bars that I ordered the Boy to take up and carry to St Margaret's church. I also snatched a leathern bag in which to carry the bones of John Paston. I had already taken a dark Lanthorn from the rectory kitchen and had ignited the candle within it from the fire there.

'What if the old boy's just a-moulderin' dust?' asked the Boy, maliciously, as we walked along the horseshoe-lane to the churchyard.

'Then we'll shove the Foulness into the bag and take that to Bacton instead,' I muttered.

The Lad snorted. Insolently, I thought.

The church was, as I knew it would be, unlocked.

We found the Table Tomb. The Boy was keen to smash it into a thousand pieces, but I took charge of the tools myself to prise away its constituent slabs. These we laid neatly in a pile before levering up the stones of the ground.

'Now,' I said to the Boy, handing him the spade, 'dig, you scoundrel.'

The Lad set to. It was an Eerie thing to watch him work by the flickering Light, and to see around us, as I moved the Lanthorn from one place to another, his grotesque Shadow gyrate upon the Altar, the Table Tombs and the great Jacobean monuments.

After minutes of grunting and cussing, the Boy cried, 'I hears the chink o' bones, Mr Cambridge Man.'

I opened the shutters of the lanthorn, and lowered it into the open pit. Yes, I could see the whiteness of a skull, the curves of shoulder blades, several long bones.

'In the bag with 'em,' says I, holding out the satchel.

The Boy was reluctant to search through the soil with his Fingers, but I threatened him with an Iron Bar; and he complied after uttering two or three Profanities.

'That'll cost you another threepence,' he muttered.

Once satisfied that the Youth had retrieved all that remained of the old Knight of the Shire's skeleton, I bade him put the pieces in the Satchel and then collect the Tools.

'Now, take me to Bromholm Priory,' I ordered.

It was a walk of about three-quarters of an Hour to that part of Bacton in which the ruins of the monastery stood.

'Up 'ere,' said the Boy, pointing to the gaunt fragments of a gatehouse tower down a side lane off the main coast Road. 'This be the biggest bit. The old abbey church, that be just a few lumps o' stone, further down this 'ere track and off to the side there.'

'Take me to the eastern end,' I commanded. 'I want the Choir.'

The boy ushered me into the ruined gateway. He stepped in behind me.

The moment we were beneath the Stone Arch, we found ourselves wrapped in what I can only Describe as a dense sea-fog.

'What the Devil?' cries I.

'Mister, which way is out of Here?' splutters the Lad.

I was disoriented myself by the Thickness of the Mist, which felt to my skin like so many Fingers of Ice trying to slice into it.

'Just step backwards,' cries I.

'I can't,' wails the Boy. 'I can't move 'em.'

My own legs had become leaden too.

The mist suddenly turned milky in appearance. Moonlight must have been piercing it, for in the fog I could see long - disembodied - fingers making for my face.

The Malevolent Spectral Digits plucked at my ears, nose, lips, teeth.

I snapped my mouth shut, and tried to take a step back. I could now Move; but the sudden and unexpected Freedom to do so made me fall backwards uncontrollably.

My poor Rump crashed onto the Track.

I called, urgently, 'Boy!'

The Youth, responding to my summons, tumbled down beside me.

We both lay there, resting on our Elbows and staring in Utter Bewilderment at the rotating, pulsating fog that coiled above us in Ceaseless Turmoil. From this weird vapour emerged Accusing Fingers, and the Palms of Hands raised up like Shields.

'Come, Boy,' I muttered, clambering up.

We fled as if the Devil himself were gnashing at our Heels.

'Where to now, Mister?' gasped the Boy. 'Back to Paston church?'

'No,' says I. 'We must hide the bones in an Obscure Place, a place where I can find them again without risk of discovery. In the corner of some remote Field, maybe; a Shady Spot under cover of trees.'

'Aye, and Tree Roots to dig through,' complained the Boy.

'You'll be paid handsomely for your Efforts,' I retorted.

'It don't be money that bother me,' shivered the Boy. 'It be ghosts n' demons. What was it as touched us, eh? Answer me that, Mr Cambridge man. Eh?'

'A Repulsive Force,' was all I could find to say.

I was trying not to shriek myself at the Remembrance of the Thing.

'Pah!'

After some Random walking, we found a small Triangular Field just to the South of Paston Hall, the Borders of which seemed to offer a cunning man good places for Hiding old John Paston's bones. Starting from the Corner angle nearest to the old Paston family residence, the Boy and I walked fifty paces down the left-hand side of the Field and buried the bones under an Ash Tree.

We snuck back into the Rectory. The Old Gentleman was still snoring by the Dining Room fire, so I picked up my Bag from the Hallway and fled back North Walsham, from which, after break of day, having Paid Off the Lad for his services, I found a coach that took me on the start of my journey back to St Peter's College.

I have been back in College for five weeks now. That Dead Gentleman, John Paston, has Appeared before me several times, increasingly Furious and Threatening, with much ranting and Shaking of Fists. But he is quite Powerless. I made trial of whether he had any Solidity, and found that he was wholly Insubstantial. Aye, I was able to push my arm through his Belly and Face, and felt no Resistance whatever. Indeed, I took to putting my feet and legs inside his Entrails for mine own Entertainment, and Dancing on his Bowels, to his evident Distress and Consternation. But he is quite Immaterial; what Mischief can he hope to Execute upon me?

Signed : *William Bodkin*

***

I met Percy Crabbe, the Perne Sub-Librarian, for a light lunch in his rooms in Peterhouse's First Court immediately after reading these bizarre documents.

Percy inhabits the set of rooms once occupied by Thomas Gray, the author of that mournful poem, *The curfew tolls the knell of parting day*. Crabbe shows none of the melancholy that was characteristic of his distinguished predecessor. In fact, he is more like the practical joker whose false cry of fire in the small hours led Gray to drop from his window, by rope ladder, and dressed only in his nightgown, into a carefully placed tub of cold water in Trumpington Street. Gray was so outraged by this base trickery that in high dudgeon he moved across the road to Pembroke College – permanently.

'Tell me about William Bodkin,' I said, as Crabbe handed me a dry sherry.

'Ah, yes. He met a strange end, if I remember right.'

Crabbe took down a smartly bound volume, *Annals of the Scholars of Domus Petri*, from his shelves, and flicked through its pages.

'Here we are,' he announced. 'William Bodkin, Scholar of Peterhouse, matriculated 1732, Bachelor of Arts 1735, Master of Arts 1738, Holy Orders 1739, Rector of Pudsey in the West Riding of Yorkshire 1740. Best known for his translation of Gregory of Nyssa's text, Λογος εις τους κοιμεθεντας, *Concerning those who have died*. Kept bees and brewed beer; *nota bene*, the famous 'Falneck Honey-Beer' named after his Yorkshire estate. Found dead 1744, chest torn open & heart half-eaten. Coroner, open verdict.'

'Good Lord!' I cried. 'That puts a sinister complexion on things!'

'Doesn't it!' chimed Crabbe.

My friend picked up Bodkin's manuscript again and scanned it rapidly.

'What,' said I, 'could possibly have broken open his chest and devoured his heart?'

'A criminal lunatic? Or perhaps something altogether more esoteric? Look here, I think we should investigate this business, Monty. Surely, there must be a link between Bodkin's record of his bizarre experiences and the even more bizarre manner of his death? What do you think?'

'I think you're keen to make a sensational name for yourself as an archaeologist!'

Crabbe laughed immoderately.

'Goes without saying, old man. But look here, you're just as keen as I am to find the old boy's bones. Don't deny it, Monty! I know you are!'

I groaned.

'But I have pressing duties at the Fitzwilliam.'

'Your faithful assistant Chapman can take care of them! You know that Something's calling you to Norfolk, don't you?'

Crabbe's green eyes glinted and gleamed at me.

'Oh, very well,' I sighed. 'When should we go?'

'There's no time like the present,' said Crabbe.

'Tomorrow?'

'And tomorrow, and tomorrow,' he added, wryly.

'Creeps in this petty pace from day to day,' I laughed.

'To the last syllable of recorded time.'

'And all our yesterdays have lighted fools the way to dusty death,' I concluded.

'Pessimist,' said Crabbe, poking me in the ribs.

I'm all for a bit of ragging, but he gave me one heck of a bruise.

Wednesday 13th September 1899

We had to change trains at Ely and Norwich, and then take a walk of about fifteen minutes from Knapton & Paston Station to St Margaret's Church. The lane led us past great fields of rolling arable land and several small copses of elm, oak, beech and ash. To the north, the sky had the brilliancy that comes from the sea being only just beyond the horizon.

Paston church is a pleasant building of the Decorated period - a fine thatched roof, scissor-braced on the inside – very rare – and a good fifteenth century rood screen; though I have to say, the interior is rather dank, with a dull green moss growing between the floor tiles.

The chancel contains two splendid funerary monuments by the Jacobean sculptor Nicholas Stone: one to Lady Katherine Paston (died 1628) and the other to her widower, Sir Edmund (died 1632). The lady's is an ornate and to my taste rather sickly pink-and-white confection, bearing an epitaph composed by the celebrated metaphysical poet, John Donne; the knight's, by contrast, is plain, sombre and depressing.

There are several table tombs in the chancel. None bears a name, though some have evidently borne heraldic shields in the past. Tradition has it that the tomb closest to the eastern end is the one that was originally erected over John Paston's grave at Bromholm Priory, and was brought to St Margaret's, along with the last remains, at the Dissolution.

Happening to glance up at the south wall of the chancel, I noticed a funeral hatchment for Sir Edmund Paston, which featured a griffin atop a crest of six fleurs-de-lys.

I grabbed Crabbe's arm.

'Look,' I said, pointing at the griffin.

My friend whistled quietly.

'Half lion, half eagle,' he said. 'Quite the beast for killing William Bodkin.'

The air in the church seemed to grow appreciably colder.

'"Saul and Jonathan were lovely and pleasant in their lives, and in their death, they were not divided,"' I recited, '"they were swifter than eagles, they were stronger than lions."'

My voice echoed around the church; and amid the reverberations, I detected a second voice, fainter than my own but harsher, muttering some of the equivalent words from the Vulgate: 'aquilis velociores, leonibus fortiores'.

'Well, well,' whispered Crabbe, cocking an ear.

I stared at him uncertainly.

The muttering in the air faded away.

'Perhaps the text describes the spirit of the Paston family,' I ventured.

'Swifter than eagles, stronger than lions?'

'We might be meddling in something we ought not to.'

'Now, look here, Monty,' asserted Crabbe. 'Don't be a pessimist. We are scholars, you and I, innocent of base motives, seeking to only to add to the sum of human knowledge. What can be dangerous about that?'

I pulled down the left side of my face.

'You can be such an old woman at times,' laughed Crabbe. He poked me in the ribs with an index finger. I flinched. I was still bruised. 'Now, come on, we need to find this field where Bodkin buried Jolly John's remains.'

We left the church and walked to the lych gate at the south-west corner of the graveyard. This opened up not onto a road – the result, I believe, of a medieval dispute in which one of the Pastons diverted the highway from the south to the north side of the church – but onto a path that ran across the front gardens of Paston Hall.

I hesitated at the Hall boundary, loath to trespass on this private space; but Crabbe marched over the gravel and along the flower beds until he came to the leafy lane that led from the coast road down to Paston Green and Knapton.

'Come on, Monty.'

I made my way between box hedges and noticed a mulberry tree on the lawn.

Crabbe was consulting his notes when I caught up with him by a hawthorn hedge.

'The triangular field is down here on the left,' he announced.

In fact, the field started just beyond the hedge.

We quickly found Bodkin's starting point, and walked fifty paces in the direction he had specified. Alas, there was no solitary ash tree to tell us we had reached the makeshift grave but rather a copse of several species. It was far from clear as to where we should dig.

'How tall was Bodkin?' I asked.

Crabbe shrugged his shoulders.

'Well, let's assume that he was five feet six inches tall,' I suggested. 'That's reasonable for a well-fed man in the early eighteenth century. It's also roughly your height, so our best guess would be fifty paces of your Crabbe legs.' Much merriment at this.

'So, we're in roughly the right place.'

We decided to dig three short trenches across Crabbe's trajectory, if necessary, one centred on the spot where my friend had stopped, one slightly behind and the other slightly ahead. But our labour was happily cut short when we discovered a leather bag in the first trench we dug, about a foot to the left of Crabbe's course.

The bag was buried a little over two feet beneath the grass verge of the field. Opening it cautiously, we beheld a jumble of old, brittle and fragmentary human bones.

Crabbe took a measuring tape from his pocket, and proceeded to jot down descriptions of what were almost certainly John Paston's remains.

'I wish I had my camera with me,' he complained. 'Very slipshod, but needs must.'

'You can take them back to Cambridge and photograph them there. Eventually you'll have them reburied in Paston church, I suppose?'

Crabbe stared at me. There was a strange light in his eyes.

'Come off it, Monty! You're as feeble-minded as Bodkin!'

'How do you mean?'

'We should return these bones to their resting place in Bromholm Priory.'

'Why on earth should we do that?'

'You read Bodkin's memorandum.'

I paused.

'The treasure story? Surely you don't believe that?'

'Of course I do. Why, the poor man had made careful preparations for the repose of his soul, at vast expense — ten oxen, twenty-two sheep, forty-nine calves, thousands of eggs, eight gallons of cream and all that – so don't you think he'd have put a little stash aside somewhere, just in case he needed to appear and bribe some living person, *post mortem*, to put right any wrong done to his remains by wicked folk like the running dogs of the avaricious Henry VIII. Eh?'

'But don't *you* think we'd encounter the same obstacles as Bodkin did?'

'I think Bodkin's brain was most likely overcome by the wine he'd drunk with Mr Jones the Rector of Paston. Besides, we shall return the remains in daylight, not darkness; and to make doubly sure, we won't enter by the old gatehouse.'

I was dubious as to whether this would be enough to divert any malign spirit, and noted that Crabbe, from his turn of phrase, was not himself wholly convinced of the safety of this enterprise either; but I was reluctant at this point to enter into controversy over what I sensed was perhaps a waxing obsession on his part.

'Hardly good practice to rebury the remains before recording them properly,' I murmured.

'It will conserve them in the very same conditions that they've been in for the last four hundred years and more,' countered Crabbe.

'I very much doubt that,' I retorted.

'They spent more time in the soil of the Priory than here.'

A specious argument. Conditions can vary greatly over small distances.

'Don't we need to tell the coroner?' I tried.

This put an end to my friend's tolerance.

'Of course not,' he snapped.

***

Bertie Morris, the owner of Priory Farm, stood hesitating at his door, bemused by Crabbe's application to return John Paston's remains to the old Choir. He wasn't sure that he wanted the bones back in his field, but when Crabbe mentioned the possibility of a treasure being found under his soil if we excavated there, he at once put his doubts aside.

'Oy, you get on wi' it, boi!' he exclaimed.

'You exaggerate,' I protested to Crabbe.

Farmer Morris's bloodshot eyes darted from Crabbe's to mine and back again. He didn't want to forego the chance of finding a hidden treasure, whether it was John Paston's or the last Prior's come to it.

'It be right, though,' he asserted eagerly, in support of Crabbe, 'puttin' the feller where he want to be. In't it?'

We set off to examine the Choir ruins. As we made our way from the farmhouse to the old cloisters, scores of crows perched in the trees around us took off with a great screaming. The sky seemed as if it were filled with pulsating deep violet-black storm-clouds. The birds' cries of alarm added to my oppression.

After some trampling around the stubble near the still clearly defined ruins of the North Transept, we located the spot where the original tomb had probably stood, in the south aisle of the Choir and close to the long-vanished high altar. The documentary sources say merely that John Paston's grave was in a Choir aisle, but the fact that his tomb was reconstructed along the south wall of St Margaret's chancel, with its heraldic decorations showing on the tomb's northern and western faces, indicates that it was originally by the south wall of the Choir at Bromholm too.

'Yes, this is the place,' Crabbe assured us, eyes agleam, looking from Ordnance map to ruins to antiquarian plan.

Our friend Bertie did the spade work; and after a short, muttered prayer from me, Crabbe lowered the skull, collar bones, femurs and other bits and pieces of John Paston that we had carried around in our bag, into the ground.

'Well, what about this 'ere treasure, then?' asked the farmer, straightening his back, after the filling-in. 'Where do it be?'

'Ah, that is a puzzle to which we have yet to work out the solution, my friend,' said Crabbe. 'But have faith. We need only consult the spirits.'

'Eh? The spirits? What spirits? How d' you mean?'

'Planchette.'

Farmer Morris's eyes lit up.

'Oh, I 'ave one o' they,' he said, excitedly. 'Mrs Morris, she like to play with it at Christmas, she do!'

'Then let's repair to your parlour and get some instructions!' smiled Crabbe.

My colleague turned and winked at me. He did not notice my grimace.

The parlour was evidently a room kept clean and clear for special occasions. Mrs Morris fussily ran in before us and swept the table with a feather duster, but she need not have worried; I could see my face perfectly reflected in the polished mahogany.

Onto this table, Mr Morris placed the planchette and its tablets of the alphabet.

After invoking the spirits, Mrs Morris, who assured us that she was 'sensitive', demanded to know if there was a buried treasure in Bromholm Priory.

The planchette, I have to say, is a most tedious device to use, but I gradually became more deeply engaged in the process as I realised that the mechanism was in fact spelling out a coherent message:

If ye wend South west well
Ye'll find old Woodrising;
Take ye candle, book, 'n bell,
And cross Rich's uprising.

'What on earth does that mean?' asked Crabbe.

'Don't you look at me for no answer, boi,' said Farmer Bertie, mouth agape.

'Well,' I said, 'Woodrising is a small village between Watton and Wymondham. It contains the tomb of Sir Richard Southwell, one of King Henry VIII's junior ministers. A most bizarre monument. It looks as if the cadaver is being kept behind bars in a prison.'

'Very relevant,' purred Crabbe, his eyes gleaming. 'Southwell took possession of the Holy Rood of Bromholm on the suppression of the Priory. He wrote to the King asking what he should do with the relic. There is no record of a reply. It seems clear to me that Southwell kept the gold and silver reliquary, and the fragment of the True Cross, for himself.'

'Yes, yes,' I agreed. 'Southwell was quite conservative in religion, though a loyal servant of the Crown politically. I dare say he valued the Holy Rood for its own sake and not simply as a monetary treasure.'

Crabbe nodded. 'Catholicism didn't die in the family,' he added. 'Indeed, his grandson Robert Southwell was executed as a traitor under Queen Elizabeth for being a Roman priest in England. Horribly executed.'

'So, this treasure be at Woodrising, do it?' queried Farmer Bertie, a man with eyes for the future not the past.

'Very possibly,' smiled Crabbe, glancing at me. 'But you'd better leave that investigation to us, my dear chap. I rather fear that delicate negotiations will be required down there with the incumbent and the churchwardens.'

'That might be so,' agreed the farmer.

Thursday 14th September 1899

Bertie Morris drove Crabbe and me in his trap to Paston & Knapton station. In Norwich, we hired a cab to take us to the twenty miles to Woodrising.

The Rectory was a pleasant-looking Queen Anne house of five bays, a pediment, dormers in the roof, the verticals emphasised with quoins. All very symmetrical. It struck me as rather grand for such a small out-of-the-way parish.

We walked up the steps to the red front door and knocked.

A young maid answered. She gazed at us with large blue eyes.

'Who shall I say is calling?' she asked, in a lilting voice.

'This is Dr James, Director of the Fitzwilliam Museum in Cambridge, and I'm Dr Crabbe, Fellow of Peterhouse, and University Lecturer in Archaeology.'

The Rector himself appeared a few moments later, spectacles on the end of his nose, a copy of Wisden's *Cricketer's Almanack* in his right hand.

He stared at us incredulously.

'Gentlemen,' he said, after an embarrassing pause. 'This is a signal honour. I'm a Cambridge man myself, you know. Exhibitioner of All Angels. What can I do for you?'

'Would you be so kind as to show us the inside of the church?' asked Crabbe.

'It's unlocked,' replied the Rector. 'But I'd be delighted to take you around myself.'

'We're interested in the tomb of Sir Richard Southwell,' I explained.

The Rector put on his jacket and took us over.

The most striking thing about the church is that its tower is utterly ruinous. The bells are, most oddly, housed in a thatched hut in the churchyard. The rest of the building is pleasant enough: medieval flint with ashlar dressings, a decent hammerbeam roof inside.

Southwell's tomb is on the north side of the chancel, beside the altar. The full-length effigy of the knight is of alabaster, and lies on a stone couch behind a grille of four Corinthian-style pilasters supporting an entablature. The pilasters are but a decorative frontage to a set of solid rectilinear columns, whose heaviness does indeed make the tomb look like a prison.

The knight lies there as a gisant, hands clasped in prayer.

'There's the old scoundrel,' chuckled Crabbe.

'Come, come - he was a man of some eminence,' protested the Rector. 'Rather worldly, of course, but pious in his own way - certainly towards the end of his life.'

'You may be right, sir,' said Crabbe. 'Why, Dr James here believes that Sir Richard took the Holy Cross of Bromholm with him to the grave, out of sheer old-fashioned piety.'

'Oh, really?'

'Yes, yes,' I said. 'Southwell had it in his possession, I'm sure of that.'

'But wouldn't he have handed on a treasure like that to his descendants?'

'Oh, no,' contradicted Crabbe. 'He'd want its saving power with him in the tomb.'

'A very medieval attitude, that,' laughed the Rector, nervously.

'Indeed,' I agreed. 'But Sir Richard was something of a traditionalist in private.'

'It would be a truly remarkable day for English archaeology if we could recover the Holy Rood of Bromholm,' commented Crabbe. 'And I wonder if that is a project that you'd be willing to take part in, sir? Monty and I would certainly welcome your contribution. You could be a joint author of a paper we're hoping to prepare for the Society of Antiquaries.'

There was a moment's silence.

'Well, I'm flattered, gentlemen,' said the Rector, 'but don't you think the Bromholm cross would have rotted away by now?'

'Some of it, possibly,' replied Crabbe, 'but not the precious metals. And it's likely that they'll be protecting the original relic, of course.'

'I see. So, you want to open up Sir Richard's tomb to look for this object?'

'Without disturbing the old fellow's remains, of course.'

Now that would require a miracle!

Crabbe had said too much.

'Oh, I don't know,' muttered the Rector. 'It's not a decision I can take. You'll need a Faculty from the Bishop, and the Home Secretary's licence. And I don't know that I could recommend to his Lordship that he should grant you a Faculty.'

'Oh, I understand your sensitivities,' I said, soothingly. 'Let's all put the matter to one side, and give ourselves more time to ponder upon it. The proper balance between reverence and archaeological curiosity is not always easy to determine.'

'Very wise of you, Dr James,' said the clergyman. 'Very wise. Now, would you gentlemen care to join me in a glass of sherry back in the Rectory?'

'Of course,' I smiled.

'Splendid idea,' said Crabbe.

I watched Crabbe force his mouth into an unimpressive rictus.

The Rector had a fine bottle of Hare's Sweet Oloroso which he opened in our honour. The colour was delightfully mellow, and seemed to match the afternoon sun which streamed in through the west-facing windows of the Rectory's sitting room.

A small fire burned in the grate.

'Just to take the autumnal chill off,' said the clergyman.

'Splendid sherry,' I remarked.

'Do you think we're heading for war in South Africa again?' asked the Rector.

'Heavens,' I replied. 'What a question! I don't know.'

'Oh, I don't like Mr Chamberlain's energetic ways,' remarked Crabbe. 'There's something almost demonic about him, don't you think?'

'He's certainly being provocative, demanding voting rights for our fellow Britons in the Transvaal,' remarked our host. 'More wine, Dr James?'

'Don't mind if I do, sir.'

Crabbe rose from his chair.

'If you'll excuse me for a moment,' he murmured, 'I must go and have a word with the cab driver - he'll be getting impatient.'

The Rector filled my glass.

'I buy my sherry from a firm of vintners in Norwich, Messrs Bonfield & Self,' he said. 'This one has a wonderfully rich flavour, don't you think?'

'Indeed.'

'Try a glass of my tawny port.'

'Goodness! It will take me a while to finish this glass!'

'Oh, just sample them.'

'Well, if you insist!'

'I'm sure you must have some marvellous single-vintage Colheitas at King's, but I hope you find this one' – he handed me a glass of port – 'a decent blend for a country parsonage?'

I tasted.

'My dear fellow,' I cried, 'this is wonderful, quite wonderful.'

'Not too nutty, is it?'

'Why, no, it's perfect.'

'Good of you to say so,' beamed the Rector. 'I was reading an article of yours in the *Contemporary Review* the other day, Monty – you don't mind if I call you "Monty", do you?'

'Not at all!'

'Excellent! Yes, I was reading your piece on the "New Sayings of Christ". Very interesting, of course, but I'm sure there's a reason why the Oxyrhynchus papyrus has been lost for nearly two millennia. Still, I think you're right about the saying, "Raise the stone and there thou shalt find me; cleave the wood and there am I."'

'Oh?'

'It's all about making an effort to find Christ, something we Church of England men have always understood, eh? Unlike the more extreme Protestants.'

The conversation was threatening to become theological.

'Are you a regular reader of the *Contemporary Review*?' I asked.

'Oh, I look at it when I have a little time to spare, I just dabble, you know. I spend most of my time managing a little bit of woodland down the lane and fishing in the rivers and ponds hereabouts. Otherwise, my days are taken up with writing sermons. And with being a good shepherd. The latter is more of a pleasure than a duty, I have to say.'

'My father has enjoyed a long career – if that is the right word - as Rector of Great Livermere in Suffolk. He is a cheerful pastor, but the point of his life has always been to preach. "It is God's great ordinance for saving souls," he says to me. Time and again!'

'Speaking of time,' said the Rector, taking out his watch, 'where is Dr Crabbe?'

'He's probably controverting with the cabman over the fare.'

'I hope he's not trying to find a way into Sir Richard's tomb.'

I laughed. 'What could he possibly do in so short a time?'

'I noticed a certain zealotry in his eye.'

'Merely a reflection from your fire, I'm sure.'

'I'll see what he's up to,' insisted the Rector.

***

I followed the clergyman through the church porch and heard him cry, as soon as he was in the nave, 'What the Devil do you think you're doing, sir?'

Crabbe and the cabman were using a couple of crowbars to lever up the base of Southwell's tomb from its foundations in the earth. The cabbie had just pushed in a log to keep the stone up. Crabbe was sliding a lighted match into the aperture with his right hand, so that he could inspect the inside of the tomb.

'Oh, damnation,' he muttered, noticing the Rector out of the side of his eye.

Crabbe turned his face towards us and opened his lips to speak; but in a flash, his frustrated, irritated look collapsed into one of sheer panic.

'For God's sake!' he screamed.

He tore his hand away from the aperture and held it up.

A swarm of blood-red spiders - each one a ruddy sixpence with legs - wriggled furiously, digging their claws and fangs into Crabbe's hand, sawing at his flesh with their maxillae.

'Get them off me!' he cried.

He battered his hand against the chancel wall so forcibly that great chunks of render clattered to the ground. His violence, his shrieks, had no effect on the spiders.

I seized the box of matches, struck one, and held the flame to the spiders; but they ran away over the surface of the hand, leaving a circle of bare skin that the flame scorched.

Crabbe swore profusely. I threw down the match.

My friend waved his hand around near his face, staring at the invaders. This was a mistake. The spiders jumped onto his top lip and, forming first into a horrid writhing moustache, began to swarm up his nostrils.

I have never heard coughing like the staccato bursts that Crabbe emitted.

The poor fellow started to beat his head against the wall. His eyes turned up into his skull, the pupils and irises disappearing completely. I shouldn't have thought that possible.

Crabbe crumpled to the stone floor, convulsing and groaning.

The cabman was frantically searching every part of his own body, but the malign spirit that had lordship of the arachnids was not interested in him.

'We must get the poor fellow to a hospital,' I cried.

'Of course, of course,' agreed the Rector.

The good shepherd's anger had given way to dread.

I cajoled the cabman to take Crabbe and me to the Norfolk & Norwich Hospital, his reward to be an escape from prosecution for as many crimes as I could remember the name of.

The Rector and I shoved Crabbe into a corner of the vehicle. I sat down opposite my friend and we sped off, leaving the astounded Rector behind.

The irises and pupils of Crabbe's eyes gradually returned to human view.

The fellow was looking around, fearful of something in the cab.

I could see nothing else with us.

Crabbe constantly repeated certain words to himself. I could not make them out at first. He spoke in a tiny whisper. At some hazard to my own safety, I placed my ear next to his mouth. Then I recognised what he was saying.

'Homo peccati; filius perditionis.'

'The Book of Thessalonians!' I cried. 'The man of sin, the son of perdition.'

Crabbe stared at me.

'Who is the man of sin?' I asked.

Crabbe gibbered, trembled, his eyes swivelling from left to right and back again.

'Who?' I cried, seizing him.

This action elicited a spray of spittle that was too much for me. I retreated to the opposite corner of the cab, wiping my face and hands, jacket and waistcoat, with a handkerchief.

I threw the handkerchief out of the window.

At the Hospital, Crabbe made a dash for the lavatory. He thrust his head deep into a toilet bowl and reaching up his arm, flushed water over himself.

With the help of a medical man, I hauled the poor fellow up again.

'Filius perditionis!'

Crabbe would not stop shouting those words, as we held him.

Then he bit his tongue so hard that blood flowed down his chin.

Friday 15th September 1899

The terrible powers of the men who dissolved the monasteries do not seem to have been extinguished by death. I'm sure that any prudent man who has experienced what I have these last few days would agree with me. I must go back to Bacton and cajole Bertie Morris into helping me return old John Paston's remains to the field where Crabbe and I found them. He knows how to handle a spade better than I. Returning the remains to Paston Hall is surely the only way I can get relief from this oppressive weight that is crushing my poor frame.

***

As I walked up the lane to Priory Farm, I could see Bertie Morris ploughing the field that lies just to the east of the old Choir. The ruins of the north transept obscured my view of him from time to time, as he moved back and forth with his plough and two horses, but I noticed, whenever I could see him, that he was repeatedly glancing behind him, his brow increasingly furrowed.

'Hallo there!' I cried from the track, when I was roughly in line with the old nave. From there, I could clearly see Morris and his horses coming back towards the place where the high altar would have been from the northern edge of his field.

Morris saw me, raised an arm in silent salute, and glanced behind him again.

The horses plodded towards me. They seemed to be shaking their heads.

Morris walked behind his plough.

One of the horses gave a snort, and faltered a little. The other one carried on.

'Hey!' cried Morris, waving his arms, objecting to the turn this put on the plough.

The horses resumed their proper course, but now both slowed down.

'Go on!' shouted Morris.

They were only about twenty feet from where the old altar had stood.

Both horses emitted a long low squeal.

'Calm down,' called the farmer.

Morris began to walk forward to his beasts, past the plough, but they bolted and, in making a sharp turn back to the northern end of the field, knocked the poor fellow flat on his back.

More squeals of terror from the by now frenzied animals. They executed a second sharp turn, and, drawing what began to look like a figure of eight on the soil, pulled the blades of the plough right over Farmer Morris's thighs, stomach and throat. He screamed in pain.

I turned my eyes to the ruins around me. I studied the mortar around the stones intently. But I could not stop myself from looking at Farmer Morris again. He was on his knees, swaying, blood pumping out from a deep gash in his neck. The thundering horses bore down on him a second time, quite demented by some inaudible voice which they had no choice but to obey.

I closed my eyes.

I waited till the screaming stopped.

I waited until the sound of the hooves faded away.

Reluctantly, I admitted the light back into my eyes. Light? More like Milton's darkness visible, I think. What I saw was indeed a product of darkness. I saw Bertie Morris lying by the old high altar of Bromholm Priory, quartered, as if by a hangman's axe.

And I could swear that I heard a sniggering in the gusting of the wind.

***

My first reaction was to vomit.

My second reaction was to do my duty as a civilised man.

I took off my overcoat and threw it over poor Morris's remains. The coverage was not perfect but it was decent enough. Then I strode off to the farm house to break the heart of poor Mrs Morris.

'I must go to 'im,' she cried, reaching for a shawl.

'No, no, you mustn't,' I insisted, taking hold of her arm.

She subsided into tears.

'Is it really so gruesome?'

I nodded unhappily.

'Is there a man you can send for a constable?' I asked.

'Jacob,' she whispered. 'He's out the back.'

The woman's legs gave way. She dropped onto a hard chair.

I found the labourer sharpening tools in an outhouse and sent him off to the coastguard cottages. He could put through a telephone call from there to the police station.

Back in the living room, Mrs Morris was weeping softly.

I seated myself on a chair at the other end of the sideboard, and pondered on the unpleasant situation in which I found myself. I seemed to be in a dilemma. How I wished that I had not fallen in with Crabbe's boyish plans to exhume John Paston's bones.

This is how the perishing business seemed to me:

If I move the bones back to the triangular field in Paston, which, I am told by local people, is called The Duffus, John Paston's ghost will come after me. Was Thomas Bodkin destroyed by a griffin? That is to say, by some vengeful supernatural entity that desired to make marks on the poor fellow's corpse suggestive of the heraldic beast of the Pastons?

If I leave John Paston's bones where they are, in the ruins of the Choir of Bromholm, then the irate spirits of King Henry VIII's Commissioners for the Dissolution of Monasteries will make merry at my expense. I do not fancy being quartered like poor Morris.

What to do?

'Would you mind if I lighted my pipe?' I asked Mrs Morris.

The kind lady shook her head, and I took refuge in a bowl of good Balkan Sobranie.

Does Crabbe's fate fit into my scheme of a *post mortem* war between John Paston and King Henry VIII's commissioners?

Maybe the invasion of Crabbe's cranium by spiders was merely an occult defence which that vicious schemer Sir Richard Southwell had put in place to protect his own tomb from grave robbers? I say 'merely', but am I mistaken in downplaying the importance of pure greed in this business? Yes, to be sure, the King's Commissioners had a liking for inflicting pain and humiliation on men and women who were perhaps too comfortable in their cloisters; but at bottom, were they not motivated more by their own love of gold and silver?

Now here we have the key, surely?

The Entity that quartered Farmer Morris is one of the King's Commissioners and is motivated by anger that he did not profit sufficiently from the spoils of the Dissolution. Yes, yes, that seems right.

How can I save myself from similar ill-treatment? Is there anyone whom I can call upon to help me?' Other than the obvious. 'Keep me as the apple of thine eye, hide me in the shadow of thy wings,' I murmur, incessantly.

Whom is it that I need to placate? Is it Southwell? Or Legh? Or Layton? Can I placate them all? But how can I do that?

I pour water into a glass on the sideboard and reflected in my drink I see eyes staring at me from behind. Hard not to drop the glass in sheer fright.

But which commissioner? Legh? Layton? Southwell? The last was a minister of the crown rather than a commissioner. Oh, never mind these scholarly niceties.

A man's life is at stake.

I cannot decide.

I would venture that it is not Southwell, or I should have gone the same way as Crabbe. That's a good point.

So, Layton or Legh?

But why would they be so vexed by a poor haul after all these centuries?

Their descendants! Aye, there's the rub.

Let me think. Layton seems not to have had any descendants at all. Legh did, but whether the line died out or still exists, I do not know.

Yes. It is either Layton or Legh, the men who visited Bromholm Priory. And if I have to make a wager over my immortal soul, I will go for Legh.

I must find a descendant of Legh and make some recompense.

Those hard men of King Henry's reign, they had all the rude vigour of the ancient Israelites, for whom an eye for an eye and a tooth for a tooth was the norm.

I hear breathing, purposeful breathing, as if making ready to exert energy in striking some fearful blow. A closeness of breath, of foul breath, the stench of decay. The air of the breath is tickling the skin of my cheeks. Sickeningly.

Mrs Morris is sitting silently, eyes closed.

Who prowls around me invisibly?

What should I do with John Paston's bones?

I am seized with an answer to this question. It comes to me like a revelation, like the rising of the sun at the end of a long cold winter's night. Why, the thing is obvious! The bones must stay here in the sacred ground of Bromholm Priory. To move poor John in the first place, though done by his own family, out of motives of decency, was to interfere unnecessarily with the sacred past.

We must always respect each fragment of the mosaic, the burial and the exhumation.

Yes, that's right.

Thursday 28th September 1899

I have settled back into my rooms at King's.

I am not, however, at ease. I have not been able to find any descendant of either Legh or Layton to whom I might pay compensation for taking John Paston's bones back to Bromholm. I'm sure that I've chosen to follow the right course of action; but judging from the sighs and mutterings and imprecations I hear from the walls of my rooms at all times of day and night, there are spirits here unhappy with my performance. I have not yet delivered the results that these unquiet souls demand.

It is my books that are suffering more than I. They fall from the shelves suddenly. The spines of several have been badly broken. Here on my desk is *Actes and Monuments of these Latter and Perillous Days, Touching Matters of the Church,* by John Foxe, an original edition of 1563, full of horrendous stories of the Protestant martyrs, the book itself quite sundered in two by its sudden plunge from the top of one of my bookcases.

I find some refuge in making outrageous noise on my old pianoforte. The popular tune *Daisy Bell* is most efficacious at driving away unquiet spirits, I find. Especially when I sing the chorus loudly.

I light all the lamps and candles I possess at night.

But sibilant malicious whisperings persist.

And I dare not shave.

Friday 29th September 1899

The great west window of King's College Chapel is being repaired and replaced by Clayton & Bell, the celebrated stained-glass makers of Regent Street, London. It will be a most impressive set of lights when finished.

I remained in chapel after Matins this morning, pondering. Crabbe is dead. I received a letter yesterday from the Medical Superintendent of the Norwich Asylum saying that my poor friend suffered a fatal stroke. That is the outward form of his death, no doubt. But we are not dealing here with only natural forces.

I do not feel entirely safe myself.

Mysterious mutterings persist.

However, remaining in King's does give me a small sense of protection, and therefore of comfort.

One of the last sections to go in the new west window is a panel on the text of Revelations Chapter 1, verse 18: 'I am he that liveth, and was dead; and, behold, I am alive for evermore, Amen; and have the keys of hell and of death.'

Watching this panel go up adds to my comfort.

The artist is a tall fellow, Algernon Mountjoy Blount, who wears an extravagant moustache and a narrow chin beard like the great Bernini. I enjoy sitting at the foot of the window, watching this chap climb up and down the scaffolding to solder little lights into place to build up a vibrant work of art.

This section of the window shows Christus Victor, radiant in his resurrection glory, standing on the head of a serpent. I can see the image taking shape before my eyes. Utterly beautiful - even though, as yet, unfinished.

But Mountjoy Blount looks puzzled.

He is studying a piece of glass in his hand. He holds it up to an oil lamp, and then searches for a white sunbeam from the east. He frowns.

'Not quite right,' he says.

'What's the matter, my dear fellow?'

'Oh, this piece. It doesn't work as I'd intended. Too blue.'

He holds up a small lozenge of glass, clearly intended to be part of Christ's glory.

'Too blue?' I query.

'Brilliant, of course,' replies Blount, 'but not as warm as it looked in our studio.'

'I have a piece you might like to examine,' I say. 'It was originally from Bury St Edmunds Abbey. It is brilliant too, but closer to the red end of the spectrum. It was probably from the south aisle of the nave of the Abbey, and was kindly given to me by a dear lady who lives in a house on the site. She unearthed it in her garden when planting a rose.'

I returned to my rooms to find the glass.

'Well, well,' said Mountjoy Blount, taking the piece and inspecting it upon my return. 'The undertones of orange, yellow and green make this very subtle indeed. A splendid piece, Dr James, thank you.'

Old Miss Rabett, of the Bramfield Rabetts, had given me the piece for the Fitzwilliam Museum, but I felt entirely justified in donating it for use in this glorious new living work of art. The donor had kindly given me full discretion over the care of the piece.

'Well, if you're sure it's acceptable, I'd love to use it,' said Blount.

'Of course.'

'I never went to university myself,' continued the artist, 'but many generations of my family have studied here at King's, you know.'

'Yes, I recall the name Blount from our Commemoration of Benefactors service.'

'My family's links with King's can be traced back to the sixteenth century.'

'Really?'

'Oh, yes. Not under the name of Blount though. Sir Thomas Legh. We descend from him. Wrong side of the blankets, as they say.'

'Sir Thomas Legh?'

'Yes, one of Henry VIII's minions. Bare ruined choirs and all that. You know him.'

'Indeed, I do.'

My heart was pounding.

There was a sudden cry from Mountjoy.

'Look out!'

He had tripped over a lamp, and was trying not to drop Miss Rabett's piece of glass.

It fell.

I raised my hands to catch it.

I did catch it, but not before a sharp corner had nicked the skin of my wrist.

I could feel the warm blood running down my shirt sleeve.

'Dr James!' cried Mountjoy Blount, in great consternation.

He descended the scaffolding with the alacrity of a monkey and grabbed my hand.

'It's not serious,' he announced.

Taking out a clean pocket handkerchief, he soaked up some of my blood, and inspected the wound carefully.

'That will make a nice V-shaped scar when it heals,' he commented.

'V for Victor,' I said, quietly.

'What's that?'

'Nothing, nothing.'

Is it I who am the victor here? Is it not, rather, poor John Paston, whose bones have been unceremoniously bundled around the farmers' fields of North Norfolk? And which now lie in the place – unremarked, and unknown but to God and to me – where he wanted them to lie until the End of Time?'

More of a *quid pro quo*, perhaps, than a victory?

Either way, I feel free at last, by the workings of a mysterious Providence.

Printed in Poland
by Amazon Fulfillment
Poland Sp. z o.o., Wrocław